THE HAUNT

THE HAUNT

A.L. Barker

A *Virago* Book

First published in Great Britain
in 1999 by Virago Press

A CIP catalogue record for this book
is available from the British Library.

ISBN 1 86049 722 5

Typeset by Palimpsest Book Production Limited,
Polmont, Stirlingshire
Printed and bound in Great Britain
by Creative Print and Design (Wales), Ebbw Vale

Little, Brown and Company (UK)
Brettenham House
Lancaster Place
London WC2E 7EN

'At the heart of our woods still lies the germ of the great forest.'

David Russell,
National Trust Forestry Adviser

When the Griersons moved from Wimbledon to Cornwall it was more a flight of fancy than a leap in the dark. They thought they were going to a new life. 'Begins at sixty,' Owen said.

'It will be like turning a page,' said Elissa. 'We'll find a village, not touristy: it needn't be thatched.'

'Miles from a superstore?'

'Heaven!'

Owen had just retired and hoped the change might compensate for the other radical change of not having a job to go to.

They found a place inland, a few houses clustered round a church and a general store. Beyond the village was a small hotel, the Bellechasse, in a sequestered corner overlooking creeks and the bay.

At the end of an unmade lane were two bungalows, one up for sale. 'Bijou', the agent called it. They couldn't see anything gemlike about it: it was solid, slate-roofed, 1960-ish vernacular. Owen thought, What more should you expect of bricks and mortar?

'We'd be overlooked,' said Elissa.

'By one other bungalow.'

'It's too far from the shop.'

'When we can no longer drive we'll walk there hand in hand.'

She would have settled for that. When the agent prised up a corner of the lino on the kitchen floor and showed them beautiful toast-brown tiles beneath, she was quite won over.

'Of course there's the garden,' Owen said, admitting an element of doubt.

'A nice challenge,' said the agent.

'Though you drive out Nature with a pitchfork, yet will she always return. Horace, 65 BC.'

They moved in on a wet day in August. Rain was tipping down, fresher and softer rain than in SW19. Owen was pleased to see how well the gutters dealt with it. This was the first house he had owned.

'Someone's watching us,' said Elissa. 'A child.'

'The water-butt fills to a secondary tap which drains directly into a soakaway.' Owen waved to the child. 'We'll have to make ourselves known.'

'Let's not be *eager*.'

Elissa wasn't happy the first day in their new home. Owen had his finer feelings, in thirty years of marriage had learned to pick his way round hers. But the business of the bed, replacing their old double with twins upholstered in midnight blue and silver, headboards to match, easy-glide castors, which he had confidently expected to be a nice surprise, was a miscalculation. He had the beds installed and waiting when they moved in. Afterwards, he saw it her way. He always did, afterwards.

2

She stared at the beds, from the beds to him. 'Where's our bed?'

'These are ours, yours and mine.'

'What have you done with our bed?'

'The rag and bone man took it.'

'You gave our bed to the rag and bone man?'

Starting to see it her way, he started to bluster. 'We couldn't bring it here, could we? It was too big, it would be out of place.'

It had always been a wonder to him how swiftly she could dissolve into tears. To do himself justice, it only happened when she was stricken to her depths and he took care that wasn't often.

'Our marriage bed! Owen, how could you!'

He must be the only one who could – her depths went down thirty years. He found a scruple which he hadn't knowingly taken into account. Now it came usefully to mind. 'You're always saying I'm restless and keep you awake. I thought you'd like a bed to yourself.'

'I never always say anything. Certainly not about you. I don't nag, I'm not a nagging wife!'

'Of course you're not.'

'You'd tell me if I was?'

'Look, about the beds—'

'You don't want to sleep with me any more.'

He grinned. 'We might find it stimulating to change beds.'

'You mean you need a boost!' She ran from the room.

He walked through the garden. It grew breast high, so he did a breast stroke, snatching at the weeds and coming eye to eye with beetles and bugs as they went about their business. What price a wild garden? Though you drive out Nature . . . He put his fist through a cobweb with a spider enthroned. It wasn't going to work. Coming here was a mistake and they didn't have the time, or the money, for a mistake this big.

He stamped through a bank of thistles, found himself facing a fence and a child, looking over.

'Hoo,' said the child.

'We're your new neighbours,' said Owen.

'Hoo, hoo, hoo.'

It was definitely a hoot.

Elissa fretted about the cleaning. Owen said the bungalow shouldn't need cleaning since it had been redecorated throughout. She took him on a guided tour of paint splashes, fingerprints, dust heaps and cigarette butts left by the workmen.

'They were supposed to decorate the house, not defile it.' She was really wound up.

Owen said, 'We'll get help.'

He asked the woman who kept the general store if she knew of anyone who would do house cleaning. She shook her head. 'People don't want it now.' As he was going out of the door she said, 'Of course there's Mrs Latimer.'

When he told Elissa she said, 'Latimer? Is she lumpy?'

'Eh?'

'Remember that sketch Joyce Grenfell did? She was at her school old girls' reunion and nobody remembered her until she said she'd been known as "Lumpy Latimer".'

Mrs Latimer arrived on a mountain bike. She mopped

4

her armpits. 'It's my son's. I borrowed it thinking to save my legs. I could always ride a bicycle – push the pedals to move and stop pushing on a gradient and float down like a bird. A hundred and fifty quid this cost and it won't even free-wheel.'

'You were in the wrong gear,' said Owen.

'Would you like to sit down?' said Elissa.

'It's my belief we should have stopped while we still could. Now look at us.' Looking at her, Owen thought that far from being lumpy, she was shaped like a rugger ball. She directed a critical stare round the room. 'The mess we're in.'

'It's the workmen,' Elissa said, flushing.

'I'm talking about the globe. Aerosols, factory affluences, motorway madness.' Mrs Latimer sat, knees apart, affording a glimpse of navy directoire knickers. 'What have you in mind, madam?'

'Mind?' Elissa disliked the 'madam'.

'What would you want me to do?'

'Just help me tidy up.'

'Let us look at the terms of employment,' said Mrs Latimer in much the same tone as Magnus Magnusson said 'Let us look at the score-board'. 'I will come for a fixed period, to do regular household tasks at the basic rate and anything extra at a rate to be mutually agreed.'

'What's the basic rate?' said Owen.

'Five pounds an hour, six-fifty for scrubbing or getting up ladders.'

Elissa looked at Owen. 'I don't know—'

'Sort it out between yourselves. I must see about getting a grass cutter.'

'You want a sickle,' said Mrs Latimer.

He drove to a superstore which advertised as a Gardeners' Mecca. He was deeply shocked by the quantity and variety of things deemed necessary for a garden: stuff to promote growth and stuff to inhibit it, glasshouses, plastic furniture, urns, gnomes, bird-baths, strimmers, secateurs, pruners.

'I want something to cut grass.'

'Manual or propelled?' said the salesman.

'Something I can sit on and watch doing the work.'

'Electric or petrol engine?'

'I think a reaper and binder – it's very tall grass.'

The salesman did not return Owen's smile. 'We don't supply agricultural machinery. But I can show you a seventeen-inch petrol mower with a four-horsepower engine, maximum cutting width, automatic bagging—'

'How much?'

'That depends on the model. We have an easy-pay scheme: a deposit secures, thereafter monthly instalments over one year or two, whichever is convenient.'

Owen sighed. 'Show me some shears.'

Charlie Olssen was working on his favourite view across Wimbledon Common, three birch trees coming together at the edge of the pond.

He had painted them in all seasons, as cobwebs balancing a quarter-inch of snow on each twig, and in high summer had tried to catch just one of their silver shudders on canvas. They put him in mind of girls not wanting to get their feet wet.

Lumsden breathed over Charlie's shoulder. 'I seen that poster you did on the Underground. At Chalk Farm. It gets to me.'

Turning, Charlie saw a lanky youth with a pigtail, wearing a singlet and broken sneakers. Charlie said, 'I've never done a poster for the Underground.'

'I'd know your work anywhere, your name's all over it.'

'What name's that?'

The youth, who couldn't know, said, 'Girl and dolphin, woman and fish, the story of evolution.'

Someone set off the anti-theft device in a parked car. It bleeped distressfully. A man kicked the car and walked on. Charlie murmured, 'Who bends not his ear to any bell which upon any occasion rings?'

'I'm an artist too,' said the youth.

People did say that; once a woman had brought Charlie her ink-blot drawings. Lumsden had followed him home and at Charlie's door said could he come in and talk.

'What about?'

'Painting. How you do it.'

'I don't know how I do it.'

'I may be using the wrong sort of brushes.'

Charlie said, 'Primitive artists did lovely jobs with feathers and chewed sticks.'

'I can't get my colour temperatures right.'

'Experiment. We all have to.'

'What with?'

'Try mixing. Some colours are bigger than others.'

'Show me.'

'Not now. I've got to pack.'

'Pack?'

'I'm going to Cornwall.'

Next morning Charlie put his painting gear and a change of clothes in the car. Well-stacked clouds were emptying over NW3. When he switched on the ignition the engine groaned: the groans grew feebler, Charlie fancied he heard a death-rattle. He was no mechanic: the working of an egg-whisk baffled him. His diagnosis was that something must have come loose. He looked, briefly, stirred the tangle of wires with his finger, shut the bonnet and got back into the car as rain began to trickle into his collar.

Something appeared close against the windscreen – large, with a yellow halo. It dipped and swayed. Charlie made out a face distorted by raindrops. He wound down the window and Lumsden, wearing a yellow sou'wester, put his head through the opening. 'I've brought some of my paintings to show you.'

'Sorry, I haven't time—'

'They're my most recent work. I'm trying to use colour the way you and Van Gogh do – so it gets to your guts.'

Charlie said, 'I can't stop now.'

'I'll come with you and we can talk on the way.'

'No one's going anywhere until this car starts.'

'Let me give it a shove,' Lumsden said obligingly. He stowed his pack on the back seat and went round to the rear of the car. Charlie released the handbrake. The car's front wheel was against the kerb. He shouted, 'Push!' Pulling on the steering, he managed to free the front wheel and the car moved. Being on a down gradient, it started to roll, picked up speed. Charlie engaged gear. The engine roused, sluggish but self-motivated;

8

the car completed the downhill run and began to struggle up. Came a cry from behind. Charlie put his foot down, switched on the wipers and was away with a splutter and a cough, the rain reducing to a clear fan on the windscreen.

Driving along Tottenham Court Road he spared a thought for Lumsden. It had been a narrow escape, but as someone said, if you answer every call for help you say goodbye to a life of your own. And he needed to think. He should have done it before setting out. Faced with the stern realities of a two-hundred mile drive in a dodgy car, already it was looking like weakness which had got him going.

He stopped for breakfast at a roadside café. It was crowded, but at one table a girl sat alone, reading. He said, 'Do you mind?'

She shrugged. Charlie swept crumbs off the chair and sat down. She said, 'Are you following me?'

'Well, no.'

'You waved to me on Battersea Bridge.'

'I came over Putney Bridge.'

'And tailed me from Barking. In a red Volvo.'

'My car's a blue Escort. I haven't come from Barking.'

She laid down her book, an Erle Stanley Gardner, and looked at him.

Charlie looked at her. By the way she had put on eye-shadow and tied up her head in a spotted kerchief he would have said she was hippie. Her skin was covered in freckles, a golden confetti concealing all evidence of character and experience. A perfect camouflage of a human face.

The waitress came for his order. He said, 'Bacon, sausage, mushrooms, toast—'

The girl interrupted. 'Was it an excuse to get into conversation?'

'Mushrooms are off,' said the waitress.

'Tomatoes, then. And toast and tea. We're into conversation,' he said to the girl. 'What do you want to talk about?'
He was reminded of Lumsden and his colour calories. It
would cost a fortune to post back his canvases and anyway
Charlie didn't know his address.

'You talk,' the girl said, 'I'm a good listener. Like the cats.'

'What cats?'

'I have a postcard of three French cats with their paws folded,
looking at the camera. The caption says it's more important to
listen well than talk well. The cats are listening, but each cat
has a different expression: one's doubtful, it's saying, "Do you
really think so?" The next one's resigned, says, "I suppose that's
true." The third's superior – "I have always known it."'

'Why French cats?'

'All cats are smart, French cats are smartest. And the caption's in French. "*Bien écouter importe plus que bien parler*".'

She took her finger off the Erle Stanley Gardner and it
promptly shut. 'Softbacks will be the death of literature. Shall
you read a book if you have to sit on it to keep it open?'

'I only read the *Digest*.'

'I'm talking about *books* – classics, Eliot, Austen, the
Brontés . . .'

The waitress brought his breakfast. He poured the last of
a bottle of brown sauce over his plate and speared a sausage.
'So why aren't you reading *Wuthering Heights*?'

'I've read it.'

'We had it as holiday reading at school,' said Charlie. 'When we asked what a wuther was the teacher said it was a powerful emotion.'

'She was right. It's from the Old Norse for a strong wind, a violent blow, a trembling. It's the heart of that story.'

'One of the kids, a wide boy, said, "Have you ever had a wuther, miss?" She went scarlet and we all giggled.'

The girl smiled, scooped the Erle Stanley Gardner into her shoulder bag and stood up. As she walked away Charlie saw that she was wearing Bermuda shorts with the recurring motif of a woman cuddling a big bird.

The farther west he went, the more conscious he would be of Nina. After Basingstoke was virtually her territory now. Marriage had made him an adjunct. He had supposed it came of being in love, a defect of the quality. But Nina had a chronically enlarged heartscape: people were tempted to disburden in her presence and he had tired of coming last in the procession of strangers' intimate splendours and miseries. Their own – his and Nina's – would have been enough, and towards the end of his married life he suspected that the constant reminder of how much worse off other people were was for her a source of strength.

That and other gnawing doubts had grown into a disquiet which even the good things about his marriage could not quell. And there were many good things.

He had Nina's portrait in the boot of the car, a full frontal nude. This was the first time it had left his studio. He had kept it in a cupboard, squeamish about its being seen by other eyes than his. Not from scruples, from wholly erotic considerations: memories.

Passing the turning to The London Apprentice he thought of John Opie, the 18th-century portrait painter, son of a Cornish carpenter, launched on London as the 'Cornish Wonder'. Maybe he should go and look at the place. But not now. Now he should do what he had come to do. Find her.

He remembered the name – 'Mellilot' – years ago, seeing it on a gate giving on an avenue of yews and beeches, a chiaroscuro wrought by the blackness of the yews and the jelly-green of young beech leaves. Nina had urged him to open the gate and drive through. He refused. Whereupon she had got out of the car and walked away along the avenue. The beeches, roaring in the wind, flooded her with light, and then she vanished into the webby dark of the yews. He had shouted, 'Where are you going?' She turned in a spasm of light and recited, '"Last night I dreamed I went to Manderley"' and Charlie settled down to wait.

Presently, the sky clouded over and the chiaroscuro faded. He had felt sleepy, would have dropped off, but was struck by the thickening and thinning, running out and replenishing of the darkness under the yews. It was surreptitious.

He opened the car door and called 'Nina!' and had regretted it because anyone listening now knew she was trespassing. 'VATE' was just visible on the top bar of the gate, the 'PRI' having been worn away, presumably by the chafing of a padlock and chain hanging loose from the post.

Then a car had drawn in behind Charlie's, a Mercedes with smoked windows. A Rottweiler was at the wheel, its elbow out of the driver's door, its black lips curled over palisades of teeth, jaws watering, snarling basso profundo.

Charlie's own juices had dried up. He couldn't go forward and he couldn't go back. The dog jumped out and made for him with a business eye. Panicking, he wound up his window, locked the car door, feeling like a rabbit cornered in a biscuit-tin.

The dog passed without a glance, went to the gate, leaned on it and bore it back on its shoulder until the gate stood wide open. A masterly performance. The dog then returned to the Merc, leaped in through the window and Charlie had the distinct impression that it backed the car into the road. Charlie started up and shot out round it. The Merc accelerated through the gate, rolled on, flattening dandelions and some late bluebells.

'Juggernaut!' Charlie had shouted, panicking for Nina who didn't have a biscuit-tin to protect her. The Merc disappeared round a bend.

Charlie was no hero but he knew what he must do. If he didn't do it he would have to answer to himself ever afterwards and the answer would be a big minus. He looked for a weapon to use in Nina's defence and his own, if need be. All he carried in the car in the way of tools was a jack. He had never changed a wheel in his life, the jack was rusted solid. There was nothing else to hand to ward off a pit-bull.

He was running along the track when Nina reappeared, trailing her bag through dandelions and cow-parsley in an idle way unlike her.

'Are you all right?' cried Charlie.

'Why shouldn't I be?'

'What about the dog?'

'Dog?'

'In the car.'

'Car?'

'It just went along the drive, there was a dog—'

'What's that you're carrying?'

'A jack.'

'Have we got a puncture?'

'Let's get out of here.' Charlie took her arm to hurry her. She hung back, brushing a head of ragwort with her fingertips. 'I saw no car.'

'It passed you, a two-tone Merc, with a dog driving.'

'You're crazy.' She dusted pollen off her fingers. 'I think I am too. We're both crazy.'

'I shan't feel happy until we're away from this place.'

'I shan't feel happy when we are.'

'Nina, please.'

'I've fallen in love,' she said. 'Deeply, passionately, hopelessly. But it needn't be hopeless.'

'Of course it needn't.' Charlie tried to pull her along. 'We'll talk about it over lunch.'

She shook off his hand. 'I can do something about it. I must, or I shall never be happy again.'

'I wouldn't have thought he was your type.'

'Who are you talking about?'

'The Rottweiler.' Out of patience, Charlie seized both her elbows and ran her through the gate.

It seemed she had fallen in love with a house: at the end of the drive, she said, was a 'heavenly, darling place, out of a dream, set among cedars of Lebanon and daisied lawns'

– she actually said the lawns were daisied – overlooking a pool and old statues representing the rape of the Sabines. They were covered in lichen and had no heads.

'How do you know they were Sabines if they had no heads?'

You didn't need faces to know what was going on, she said coldly. She had wanted Charlie to go back with her to look at them. He flatly refused. 'I'm not going near that dog, it's a killer.'

'There is no dog. You went to sleep and dreamed it.'

No use arguing at that juncture. He had hauled her into the car and driven away without waiting to belt up. She twisted in her seat to look back. 'I intend to have that house.'

'We can't afford it.'

'I'll marry into it.'

In fact that was what she had done, and Charlie, married to her for ten years, could well imagine how she had done it, although he was not privy to the details. When she had ascertained that Crawford, the owner of the house, was a widower, she divorced Charlie. He prophesied disaster if she wed the house and not the man. She said real estate was an investment. She was cool and businesslike. Charlie supposed that emanated from her prospective bridegroom whom she referred to succinctly as 'J.T.' Charlie was not asked to the wedding, but a woman who was told him that J.T. reminded her of Oscar Wilde. It was, she said, a passing resemblance and did not survive conversation with him.

Searching now for Mellilot, Charlie took several wrong turnings before he found the lane which led to what had become Nina's drive. He wouldn't have recognised it were

15

it not for the yews and beeches. Those she could not change. But the wild look was gone – the yellow ragwort and purple loosestrife; the surface had been Tarmacadamed, the chiaroscuro was just black shadow. 'Last night I dreamed I went to Manderley' – and tidied it up.

He turned his car in at the gate and drove on. No need to worry about the dog. Nina did not like dogs, he could rely on her prejudice.

The drive forked: to the left an archway gave on to a stable yard, to the right topiary, corkscrew hedges and privet peacocks. Beyond was the house.

Recalling Nina's rhapsodies – 'a heavenly, darling place' – he was struck, not for the first time, by shortfalls between her vision and his. To him this was strait-laced country Georgian, conceding a pediment and floral swags over the second-floor windows. Cedars there were, but the daisies had gone from the lawn. A ride-on mower was even now shaving off the last of them.

Charlie drove up to the front door. The knocker, an iron teething-ring, made a lot of noise but no one came in answer. He knocked again. A bird flew, cursing, from the eaves.

The rider on the mower called out, 'We don't want double glazing,' and made fending-off gestures.

Charlie crossed the grass. 'I'm looking for Mrs Crawford.'

'She's not here.'

'Where is she?'

'Away.'

'What about Mr Crawford?'

'I am he.'

'J.T.?'

The man on the mower pouted. Being completely bald, he looked more like a punished baby than Oscar Wilde.

'I've got something for you,' said Charlie. 'In my car. Shall I fetch it?'

J.T. Crawford shrugged and remained seated on the mower. Charlie went to his car and brought the portrait, the full frontal view hidden against his chest. 'You and I aren't complete strangers. Your wife used to be mine, we have what you could call a shared interest.' Charlie smiled friendlily. 'What does the J.T. stand for?'

'Jeremy Tyrone.'

'I'm Charlie Olssen.'

'What's that you've got there?'

'Our shared interest.' Charlie turned the picture. Looking at it upside down he thought it really rather good. Even in bright sunlight the *morbidezza* was rich and bloomy. Bedbloomy. Nina could be voluptuous when she chose, and she had chosen while he captured her pose. In the curve of her hip and upstanding breasts he saw a definite affinity with Alma-Tadema's *Tepidarium*. In place of the coy ostrich feather, affectionate treatment had been given to her pubic hair, of which she had a riotous triangle. All the salient points had been made with no loss of mystery.

Crawford took one look at the picture, ducked, and fumbled the switches on the mower.

'I want you to have it,' said Charlie. 'I painted it but it's yours by conjugal rights.' He added soothingly, 'Only you and I have seen it.'

17

Crawford kept fidgeting with the mower. His pate was the colour of port wine. 'It's suggestive.'

'I was her husband at the time.'

'People might think I did it.'

'Isn't it good enough? As a work of art?'

'Nothing personal.'

'As a picture it may not be your taste. I don't know your taste. Gothic, is it? Baroque? Landscape? Still lives – dead rabbit with oysters?'

'I've nothing against your work.' Crawford swallowed. 'It's really quite – what will you do with it?'

'I'd like you to have it. You're the one entitled now. But if you relinquish your claim I'll be free to offer it for the Academy Summer Exhibition.'

The blood rushed into Crawford's ears. 'How much do you want for it?'

'I'm giving it to you.'

Crawford climbed off the mower and went across the lawn. He disappeared through the arch into the stable yard.

Charlie followed. In the yard, paved with professionally distressed stone flags, were fibreglass urns planted with pink hydrangeas, a 1920s lamppost and a horse-trough brimfull of geraniums. In a corner stood a wagonette painted bright blue with yellow wheels.

Charlie sighed. Uncertain whether to wait or go, he perched on the footplate of the wagonette and gave himself up to thoughts of Nina.

Painting her in the nude had been a shared experience, surprising them both. He had done it at a time when they were still enveloped in each other. She had overcome her inhibitions so quickly that he had wondered if she actually ever had any. They had come back later.

In the first days of their marriage there was nothing she would not do for him, nothing of herself – her body and her emotions – which she would not show for him. In all innocence. If there was any sin in their passion it was only what other people would see in it. Life together had been as close to life in Eden as they were ever likely to get. Once, much later, he was unwise and unhappy enough to ask her if it had been as idyllic for her. He wanted to hear her say so, to admit there had been that wonderful time. But she had said, 'We were such babies,' and emptied Eden out with the bathwater.

He propped the portrait (*Nina complaisant* was how he thought of it) against the wheel of the cart, turning it to confront the fibreglass urns and the horse-trough. Crawford, coming across the yard, averted his eyes.

'What happened to the Sabines?' asked Charlie.

'What?'

'The statues that were here.'

'They weren't Sabines. It was a bacchanalia. She got rid of them.'

'Where is she, actually?'

'Westminster, lobbying an MP.'

'What about?'

'Extinction. She wants it stopped.'

Charlie laughed, Crawford glowered. He thrust a piece of paper at Charlie: it was a cheque for thirty guineas. He picked up the portrait and stared into it.

19

'Where will you hang it?'

'I shall burn it.'

'You can't do that!'

'I can, I've paid for it, it's mine to do as I like with.' Crawford's jowls trembled. 'I shall like to burn it.'

Mildred Gascoigne had brought her folding chair to an unfrequented part of the hotel garden to watch the graceful passage of white sails across the bay. But her eyes had grown heavy; she was seeing only a crow stooping about in the mud. The crow turned over the mud like a connoisseur. There was rather a smell which Mildred attributed to weed festooning the keels of some beached boats. A bitter taste in her mouth indicated that she was out of sorts. She had not come here to go through it all again, she had come for her health – a change, a rest – not anticipating the gaiety and care-freedom most people sought in a holiday. She folded her chair and made her way back to the hotel.

A girl was on the terrace, edging between the wrought-iron tables and the sunbrellas. She came to the top of the steps and looked down at Mildred. Mildred said, 'Can I help you?'

The girl's appearance was unprepossessing, not to say slovenly. It implied, Mildred thought, sovereign disregard of anyone else's opinion, but of course nowadays it was a cult with young people to make the worst of themselves.

The girl spoke without preamble. 'Who was that I just saw in a wheelchair?'

'There is a disabled gentleman staying here,' Mildred said guardedly.

'Name of Piper?'

'Indeed no!' When Mildred had asked, in the nicest possible way, who her fellow guests were, and seen his signature
in the hotel register – 'Maurice Piper' – that fine calligraphic
script, she had experienced a shock of pure joy. She said, 'Do
you know him?'

The girl shook her head. 'But he's here? Piper, I mean?'

'You must ask Mrs Clapham. She is the proprietress.'

'Who are those two wheeling the old boy?'

Mildred said sharply, 'I understand Mr Eashing is an
antiquarian. Two of the guests have volunteered to take
him for a walk.'

'Are there any rooms vacant?'

'I'm not privy to the functioning of the hotel.' Mildred
turned away. 'Enquire at reception.'

She put on her floral silk to go down to dinner. It was
suitable for a minor social occasion, and the pre-prandial
display here was not exactly dazzling. This was no five-star
hotel. The brochure described it as 'for connoisseurs of peace
and plenty, set in secluded grounds with private foreshore,
in the reaches of the River Fal, overlooking the beauty of
the creeks. A warm welcome and the finest home cooking
is assured you at the Bellechasse.'

The welcome on Mildred's arrival had been disrupted by
an argument as to which room she had been allocated. Mrs
Clapham had stalked off in a rage, leaving her husband to
carry Mildred's luggage and conduct her to her room. There
seemed to be no porter.

The room, when they came to it, was clean and homely.

You couldn't say fairer than that, thought Mildred. It looked out on a sombre assembly of rhododendron bushes. Mildred supposed it was too early in the season for them to be in flower.

Clapham had thrown open the window with a flourish. 'You can see the Sillies on a clear day,' Mildred understood him to say.

'I beg your pardon?'

'The Scilly Isles.'

'The bathroom is not *en suite*?'

'It's right across the landing, you'll be sharing with Mister Piper from up in the tower.'

Mildred felt herself flushing scarlet. Clapham grinned. 'He's not here just now, he was called back to London a couple of days after he booked in.'

'I would much prefer—'

'So you've got it all to yourself. I hope you'll be comfortable.'

'—a south-facing room—'

'All bedrooms face east,' Clapham said cheerfully. 'There's a sun lounge and a log fire in the TV room after 6 p.m. You'll be nice and cosy. Let us know if there's anything else you want.' His tone had left Mildred with the impression that it would be unreasonable to want anything else.

As she went into the dining room the young Wallingtons, husband and wife, saluted her. A middle-aged couple looked up from their soup and nodded. Mr Eashing, the antiquarian, was intent on steering his wheelchair between the tables.

Mildred was not altogether pleasantly surprised when the girl she had met on the terrace came into the dining room and stood looking round. Seeing Mildred, she came to her table. 'May I sit with you?'

'I believe the tables are numbered according to one's room.'

'Are you waiting for someone?'

When Mildred shook her head the girl pulled out a chair. She hadn't bothered to change; she wore a T-shirt and what Mildred believed were called the Bermuda shorts she had arrived in. Mildred said, 'If you sit here it will confuse the waitress.'

'Which of these people is Piper?'

Mildred experienced a sharp intestinal fuss. 'I believe he has gone to London.'

'Is he coming back?'

'He hasn't vacated his room.'

'You checked?'

Mildred said stiffly, 'I happened to hear Mrs Clapham remark on the muddle it was in.' She thought it her turn to ask a question. 'Are you staying here?'

'I've taken a room, you'll see me around.' She held out her hand. 'My name's Senga. Agnes backwards.'

'How original.' Mildred didn't feel she could say how pretty because it wasn't. 'My parents called me Mildred after a great-aunt. They hoped she'd leave me her money.'

'Did she?'

'No. She took it with her. She lived to be a hundred and the money went to keep her in a nursing home.' Mildred had found the wry little jest useful for breaking the ice.

The waitress came with soup. She set it before Mildred and stared in alarm at Senga. 'Nobody said anything about her.'

23

'It's quite all right, Bettony, this young lady is staying here. You can bring her soup to my table.'

'There's only one left, and that's Number Nineteen's.'

'I'm Number Nineteen.' Senga peered at Mildred's plate. 'I don't think I want any of that.'

Bettony cried, 'It's poured already! She won't have it left!'

Mildred said, 'Just tell Mrs Clapham the lady in Nineteen doesn't wish to take the first course.'

Bettony glared and trundled away, preceded by her bosom which was large and uncontrolled.

'She should wear a horse-collar,' said Senga.

Mildred sighed. 'Poor child.'

Senga leaned across the table, knocking Mildred's bread roll to the floor.

'When will Piper be back?'

Mildred felt the questions should add up to something. She said, 'Why do you want to know?'

'I'm a journalist, interested in people. They're my bread and butter.'

Mildred worried about the roll. It would be unhygienic to pick it up and replace it on the table.

Bettony returned with a plate of soup. 'Here's yours,' she said to Senga.

'I don't want it, I told you.'

'She'll charge you for it.'

'It doesn't matter, please take it away.'

Soup was spilled on the cloth. 'Look what you made me do!' wailed Bettony.

Mildred mopped up the soup and sprinkled salt on the

cloth. 'Salt stops discolouration. Don't worry, Bettony, we'll tell Mrs Clapham we did it.'

Bettony trod on the roll which disintegrated under her.

The next course was served in one of Mrs Clapham's scenic permutations: a quarter chicken supreme among green beans, Duchesse potatoes and florets of purple-sprouting broccoli irrigated with gravy. Mildred said, 'I always think dessert is the nicest part of a meal. Mrs Clapham makes excellent puddings, she has a light touch with pastry.' Senga, chewing a head of broccoli, seemed to be concentrating on something other than food. 'Do you like cooking?'

'I never cook.'

The first to finish her meal, she left her knife and fork askew on her plate and sat looking round the room. 'Who are those two by the window?'

'I believe they are Americans.' Mildred met her gaze. 'Which newspaper do you work for?'

'I'm a freelance.'

Mildred had visions of pennants carried into battle. 'I take the *Telegraph*. I can't always complete the crossword, but I enjoy the challenge.'

'You're not married.'

It was a statement, a conclusion reached, the knack – indispensable in her profession – of winkling out the heart of the matter: any matter.

Mildred said, 'I have chosen not to be.' One might choose without being offered a choice. 'I am singular by nature.'

'Aren't we all?' Senga reached into the air and a cigarette materialised between her fingers.

25

'The dining room is a no-smoking area,' warned Mildred. 'Mr Eashing takes his pipe into the garden.'

'Where does Piper take his?'

It was provocatively spoken, but Mildred felt it was intended to provoke a viable answer. 'I have always believed him a non-smoker.'

'*Always*? How long have you known him?'

'Just a manner of speaking,' Mildred said, flushing.

It rained steadily after the Griersons moved in. Owen put up shelves, mended a fuse, swept out the garage, wrote letters, tried to do the *Times* crossword. Raindrops, leisurely as glycerine, slipped down the grass stalks. On the third day the clouds parted, the sun came out and the garden steamed.

All their married life they had lived in flats, conversions – and for a brief traumatic period – high-rise. Owen's close encounters with gardens derived from visits to National Trust properties, and the back yard of his childhood home. He found the superabundance of Nature hard to take.

He did the shears in the garage and went exploring. At the end of the garden a paddock fence gave on to the lane. It led through mud into a fir plantation.

Under the trees was a gamey smell which pierced his sinuses. He couldn't identify it. At the side of the path he glimpsed what he took to be flowers, white roses, and thought, That's nice. But when he drew level the flowers were the feathers torn from the half-eaten corpse of a bird.

It was stock-still under these trees. Although a wind drove the clouds overhead, here below the dry twigs did not stir. But he saw something out of the corner of his eye, an extraneous flutter which ceased when he looked over his shoulder: it could have been a flash of light in his own eyeball.

The trees thinned, gave on to a field planted with low-growing green, a crop of some sort. Circling it, Owen was pleasantly surprised to come to a pool fringed with yellow irises and being musically replenished by the fall from a swift-running culvert.

He went to the brink, disturbing waterfowl which scrambled up the bank with fussy cries. Muddied, the water flowed into a still centre peppered with gnats.

In relaxed mood, Owen tossed twigs into the gnats. Some twigs fell short, interrupting the music of the little waterfall. He took a stick and worked to clear them, dislodging a big stone. The fall fell stronger. When he lifted his stick from the depths it was draped with a shawl of brilliant green weed. The voice of the fall changed to a deeper, sweeter note; suddenly the water was shooting up the sun. Splinters of light fell round him, the trees roared in the wind.

Like an ovation. Why not? Suddenly he felt wholly glad that they had come here to live. It had been a gamble, but so was everything nowadays and at their time of life they stood a greater chance of losing. He looked about to identify the factor which had resolved his doubts. There was nothing he could pass on to Elissa, he couldn't say what makes it all worthwhile is a waterhole with wildlife. As he turned to go he lifted his hand in salute, acknowledging benefit received.

On the way back he sighted someone under the trees, someone small, in a bright blue jump suit, running away.

'Little beggar must have been following me,' he told Elissa.

'Why would he do that?'

Owen shrugged. 'Kids!'

'Mrs Latimer says he's a handful.'

'If he does it again I shall speak to his parents.'

'His mother's a widow.'

It was the first he heard of her, that she was a widow, alone but for her child. He had a thumbnail view of a forlorn woman in widow's weeds and thought no more about her until he saw her hanging out washing on a boisterous September day. She was having to cling on to the clothes line to hold down sheets which were breaking out like sails. As often as she reached up to put on a peg she was engulfed, overpowered. She lost her temper, fought the wet linen, laying into it as if it was a punch ball.

Owen leaned on the fence to watch. It was as good as a variety turn, he told Elissa. He was remembering how she looked, a young woman with red hair a shade darker than poppies, putting strands of it back from her cheek.

He said, 'We should make ourselves known.'

'She should welcome *us*.'

'She probably feels a bit diffident.'

Elissa smiled. 'Redheads aren't known for their diffidence.'

It was the child who brought them together. He had found – Owen rather thought he had made – a gap in the fence and crept through whenever Owen was in the garden. He wouldn't, or couldn't, speak. In reply to Owen's questions he hooted, without mockery or intent to offend. He was able to put a degree of response into each hoot – acquiescence or denial politely conveyed. Owen couldn't be annoyed, but he did wonder.

'He must be about six years old: he should have learned to talk by now.'

'Mrs Latimer says he's a dummy.'

'I don't think that's true. It's as if he's ruled out the need of words.'

'He'll be in trouble if he has.'

As he worked, chopping off the heads of weeds, Owen tended to muse aloud, a sort of grumblelogue. He noticed the boy drawing near to listen. Translating my whingeing into hoots, Owen thought. I'll try him with something happy.

'Did you know there's a pool with a little waterfall and a posse of black ducks on the other side of the wood?'

'Moorhens,' said the boy.

'You surprise me – I thought you'd done away with words!'

He came and put his hand in Owen's. 'My name's James. Will you come with me?'

'What?'

'I'm not allowed to go there alone.'

'We'd have to ask your mother.'

Owen didn't particularly want to talk to her. She was young, and young women embarrassed him, on their account as much as his. Because he was old and big and a man, they weren't sure how to treat him. They either turned skittish and teased, tried mock flirtations, took the mickey, were insolent or – which he preferred – openly dismissive.

The colour of this young woman's hair was the sign of a temper quick to reach flashpoint – she would suspect him of indecent designs were he to suggest taking the boy into the wood.

James tugged at his hand. 'Come and ask.'

'Not now.' Owen prised his fingers free. 'I have work to do.'

Next day he drove Elissa into town. They had lunch and took in a film. When they returned home it was dark.

'By the way,' Elissa said as they turned into their drive, 'I met your boy's mother picking blackberries in the lane.'

'He's not *my* boy.'

'She says he'd like you to take him for a walk and if that's what you'd like, it would be nice.'

He said casually, 'What's she like, then?'

'Tuck that red hair under a scarf and you'd hardly notice her.'

Next day it rained again. Owen had left the shears out in the garden and went in search. James was watching through a window, flattening his nose on the glass. Didn't they go to school at his age?

A sea-mist came up overnight. The sea was miles away but it must be a sea-mist because it tasted of salt.

'No gardening today. Couldn't see a weed in front of my nose.'

'He's waiting for you. Over by the fence,' said Elissa.

Owen said, 'Damn.' When he went out to him, James took possession of his hand and tugged him towards the gate. In his other hand was a paper bag.

'What's this?' Owen feared he had brought his lunch.

'Bread for the moorhens.'

'We can't go to the pool today.' James's mouth drew down at the corners: he wasn't too old to cry. 'All right, all right,' Owen said hastily and let himself be pulled into the lane.

In the fir wood the mist was shredding, blowing in tatters through the trees. Owen was relieved to see that

30

the mangled corpse of the bird had gone; he didn't fancy having to interpret messy death to this child.

'Why aren't you at school?'

It sounded peremptory. James released Owen's hand and ran away.

'Come here!' James ran deeper into the trees, stooped to pick something up. 'Come back! Please . . .' James was carrying his hand to his mouth. Owen shouted, 'No! Don't!' and went in pursuit. He might be a townsman but he had seen fleshy growths crimped like pie-crusts and looking tasty. His ankle turned on a tree-root. 'It's fungi – poisonous – you'll die if you eat it.'

James came slowly towards him, opened his hand. There was nothing in it. Owen said sternly, 'I don't find that funny. You haven't answered my question. Don't you go to school?'

James's lip trembled; he still held the best card – tears. He lowered his head and scuffed up the pine needles. Owen took his hand and scuffed with him.

When they reached the pool it was the colour of an old penny. A steady drizzle fretted the water, the fall burst unmusically from the culvert, the irises were bowed down, moorhens put up watery cries from the reeds.

'Not the day for it,' Owen said, 'it needs the sun,' and would have turned away, but James opened his paper bag, took out a handful of bread. 'We'd better go back.'

James went to the water's edge, threw the bread. A flotilla of birds arrowed out of the reeds. He threw more bread.

'That's enough,' said Owen. 'You'll get wet.'

James stooped, uttering the same watery cries as the

31

moorhens. The water lapped over his shoes. James lost his footing and his balance, plunged forward. There was little depth so near the verge, he ended on his stomach in the shallows.

Owen ran to him. James propelled himself into deeper water. Owen was obliged to wade in up to his knees. He gripped James's shirt-collar as he started to go under, and hauling him up had the rare experience of rescuing someone about to drown and enjoying it. James's eyes, wide with surprise and pleasure, darkened with anger as he was dragged to the bank. He fought off Owen's grasp. 'I was swimming!'

Owen held him at arms' length. 'You were drowning. You're soaked to the skin and covered in mud. What am I to tell your mother?'

'I drowned.' James looked down with pride at his wet clothes.

'Let's get it right for the record; you weren't swimming and you could have drowned. Now I have to get you home before you catch pneumonia.' Owen put a hand between James's shoulder blades to start him walking. James floundered in the mud. 'Where are your shoes?'

'In the water.'

Owen picked him up. There was nothing else for it. James, in playful mood, clung around Owen's neck and huffed into his ear. When they emerged into the lane, in sight of his mother's bungalow, he threw himself full length in Owen's arms, let his head and legs hang lifelessly.

'There's no need for that.' Owen was annoyed when a passing woman stood and gaped in alarm.

James's mother's hair was what Owen believed was called Venetian red. Since she hadn't passed it on to her son and

James had a hooked nose while hers was a small snub, possibly the father's genes had prevailed. Owen couldn't accept Elissa's verdict that were it not for the colour of her hair no one would look twice at her. He, at any rate, was tempted to speculate and had been since witnessing her display of temper. A woman who could come to blows with her washing line was singular.

She looked him over, appraising, noting his mud-soaked trousers and waterlogged shoes. James hung on her arm crying, 'I drowned!'

She said sharply, 'Go and take off your wet things. I'll run a hot bath,' and turned to Owen. 'You must be very uncomfortable.'

'I'm so sorry. James was feeding the ducks when he slipped in the mud. I had to fish him out of the water.'

'I can't offer you dry clothes, my husband's wouldn't fit you.'

'No problem. I get through the fence and I'm home.'

'Of course,' she said, 'you're our new neighbour.'

A commonplace exchange. But Owen wondered. Didn't parents – mothers especially – fear for their offspring, suffer with them, forsaking all others? She had scarcely glanced at James to see what harm had come to him.

Owen changed out of his wet things and went in search of Elissa who was lying on her bed. She said, 'I have a terrible headache.'

'A migraine?'

'Another. So tedious. How was your morning?'

'Wet.'

'You exposed that child to the elements?'

'His mother didn't seem bothered.'

'Do you think these migraines could be something else? Something *more*? The symptoms aren't right. I don't feel nauseated and I don't see flashing lights. It's not a throbbing pain, it's piercing – *pressure*.' Elissa propped herself on her elbow, staring at him. 'You know what I mean?'

He knew. They had been through it so often, as often as she had a headache, a cough, collywobbles, a twinge of rheumatism, was liverish, felt dizzy, caught a common cold. He had surprised her groping herself in the bathroom. 'What on earth are you doing?' 'It's the recommended procedure to be carried out daily.' He was unwise enough to ask what she was looking for. She had told him, with a mortal fear which he had tried to laugh off. It brought on a blazing row.

'My dear girl,' he said, gently now, 'I think you're subject to nervous headaches. I shall make strong tea and bring you your pethidine pills.'

'She's asked me to go and have coffee with her.'

It was natural that couples who lived together in the same conditions and constantly faced the same situations should develop a degree of thought transference. Owen said 'She?' more from a wish to establish a name than a question of identity.

'The woman next door.'

'Shall you go?'

'Why not? You keep saying we should make ourselves known.'

*   *   *

34

'Nice enough, little Mrs Hartop,' was Elissa's verdict afterwards. 'Rather pathetic. She seems to think we're sophisticates from the Big City. The coffee was instant, in pottery mugs. The child hooted at me. She says he has a speech impediment when meeting strangers and hooting is his way of getting started. The kitchen, which was all I saw of the house, was user-friendly. Obviously it's where she spends most of her time and smokes her cigarettes. Doesn't she realise she's putting the child at risk as well as herself? Someone should take her in hand.'

'Why don't you?'

'Mrs Latimer warned me. She said the air was so polluted she was taking the fumes home on her clothes.'

'He who denigrates his neighbour bears witness against himself,' intoned Owen: something Horace might have said. He was pleased with it.

'It's common knowledge.'

'Common gossip.'

'There's no smoke without fire.' Elissa was pleased with that.

'I shall go and enquire how James is.'

'I told you, he hooted, he's alive and well.'

'I ought to show concern, he was my responsibility.'

Elissa said, 'I don't see you as a child-minder.'

When she opened the door to him she had a towel wound turban-wise round her head. Not a strand of hair showed, it was as if a shout had been silenced.

Owen said, 'I'm sorry, this is a bad moment.'

35

'It would have been ten minutes ago, but I've finished washing my hair.' She beckoned him into the small hallway. From an open door wafted the warm breath of an Aga. 'Come in.'

On the threshold of the kitchen he trod on something soft and yielding. 'Oh lord . . .' and stooped to pick it up – grey, woolly, legless, with glass beads for eyes.

'It's James's.' She took the thing, nursed it in her arms.

'I came to see how he is.'

'Excuse me a moment.'

He heard her cross the hall, the sound of a door closing, a key turned in a lock. She came back. 'Won't you sit down?'

'Is he all right?'

'He's fine. James is fine.'

'His shoes sank without trace. I'll go and fish for them.'

'Please don't.'

'My wife says children's shoes cost a bomb.'

'Can I offer you anything? Coffee? Tea?' Owen shook his head. 'Whisky?'

'Too early for me.'

'Stretch a point.' She fetched a bottle and glasses, poured a generous finger in each glass and put hers down with a single swallow. There was a hint of showmanship in the way she unwound the towel and shook out her hair. 'Why did you come here?'

'I wanted to be sure James hadn't suffered ill effects from his wetting.'

'I meant why did you come here to live?'

'Primarily to get away from London.'

She was turning her head this way and that, causing her hair to stream out like a flag. Unnerved, he took a sip of whisky.

'The people here are gossips. They spread stories about us which you may choose to believe.'

'I hope we'll be good neighbours.'

She wasn't listening, she was looking through the window. 'A policeman is coming. Oh God . . .' She sounded dismayed.

'Would you like me to go?'

'I'd rather you stayed.'

'He's probably making some routine check. Or selling tickets for the police ball.'

'Would you mind seeing what he wants?' She began vigorously towelling her hair.

Owen opened the door to an archetypal village bobby who pushed his helmet off the bridge of his nose, the better to stare at Owen.

Owen said, 'Can I help you?'

'Can I speak with Mrs Greville Hartop?'

'Angela Hartop.' She had come to Owen's side. 'My husband's name is Greville.'

The policeman had probably never seen hair of such colour and confusion. Tousled from the drubbing she had given it, it stood up in points of fire all over her head. If she wished to discountenance him she had succeeded. Flustered, he said to Owen, 'And you, sir?'

'Name of Grierson. I live next door. My wife and I moved in a week ago.'

'We were aware. Allow me to introduce myself. Police Constable Winslow of the local force. Acting on information received, I have some questions to put to Mrs Hartop.'

She said, 'What information?'

'An unconfirmed report of a man seen carrying what appeared to be a dead child.' He opened his notebook. 'Can you throw any light on that?'

'My child is not dead. Why come asking me questions?'

'The man was seen approaching this house.' PC Winslow leaned on the words.

'You see?' She turned to Owen. 'You see how the people here have taken against us?'

'The information came from a lady staying at the Bellechasse Hotel. She describes the man as elderly, tall, thickset, shabbily dressed, with glaring eyes.' Owen smiled. 'She was greatly distressed, she said the child looked as if it had been drowned.'

They heard a door-handle rattle violently and a long-drawn wail. The constable said, 'Somewhere a child is crying.'

'My son James in his room.'

'If you have no objection I'd like to see him.'

'My objection is that he'll think he can always get his own way if he makes enough fuss.'

She crossed the hall and the wailing ceased at the sound of a key in the lock. Next moment James flung himself at Owen and hugged his knees.

PC Winslow asked, 'Why was he locked in?'

'I wished to talk to Mr Grierson.'

Couldn't she see how that would be represented? thought Owen. The policeman certainly could. He sank to his heels and turned James to face him. 'Now, young man, what's up?'

'Hoo,' said James.

'You, I'm talking to you, laddie.'

'Hoo.' James made a funnel of his hands and shouted through it. 'Hoo! Hoo! Hoo!'

PC Winslow rose to his full height. 'Is he mentally retarded?'

'Look,' Owen said, 'we'd had a slight mishap, that's all. He slipped in the mud and lost his shoes. I was carrying him home.'

James spluttered with laughter. 'I drowned!'

Elissa was disposed to make light of Owen's apprehension. 'Darling, you're old enough to be her father.'

'That makes it the more titillating,' Owen said grimly.

He avoided the garden, but was conscious of James's presence. The boy must have been warned not to intrude: he put his head and shoulders through the gap in the fence and hung there, watching. It put Owen in mind of someone in the stocks.

When James had gone to bed he went out and closed the gap with a plank driven into the ground and lashed to the end posts. He felt mean doing it, and something else – a generalised discontent; throwback, he supposed, to his misgivings about the wisdom of coming here to live.

'You do realise,' he said to Elissa, 'that any malicious tittle-tattle about Mrs Hartop and me would rub off on you?'

'I've never been part of an eternal triangle: it would be quite an achievement at my age. But of course the achievement would be yours, wouldn't it?'

He left it there. Smarting, drove to a pub called the Dolly Pentreath. A pint of real ale restored him to what Horace would call an equable mind.

People were discussing how and why the pub had got its name. Someone said Dolly Pentreath was the last person to speak the old Cornish, someone else said she had been a wrecker's moll who helped lure sailors to their death. They rather thought she might have died of gin here in the bar. No one was really bothered.

Angela Hartop had just turned into their lane, walking from the bus stop, pulling a loaded shopping trolley and carrying a parcel under the other arm. There was no way he could have driven past and left her.

She was unsurprised when he pulled up beside her and waited while he put her luggage in the boot. She looked hot and tired, the faint down on her upper lip was moist, the tender skin under her eyes looked bruised.

Owen noted the details without any idea what he was going to make of them. 'I'd have offered you a lift if I'd known you were going into town.'

'You're very kind.'

'I was going anyway.'

'I think James has fallen in love with you.' Owen laughed. She said, 'It's not to be wondered at. He needs a man in his life.'

When he stopped the car at her gate she said, 'You don't want him though, do you?'

'On the contrary, I've become quite attached to him.'

'Is it your wife?'

'Elissa?'

'Is she why you closed the gap in the fence?'

'I did it because my garden's no place for a child, there are too many thistles and stinging nettles.'

She opened the car door. 'I'm obliged for the lift.'

'I know you don't like the smell of beer, it makes you sick and you're always hoping there's another reason: I know the reason,' said Antony Wallington to his wife, Pam. 'You didn't have to come on this holiday.'

'Neither of us has to do anything. It's our creed.'

'What will you have to drink?'

'A very small, very dry sherry.'

'A very small, very dry sherry,' he said to the barmaid. 'And a pint of bitter.'

She looked askance at him as she pulled his beer. 'We don't serve very small sherries. And just dry, not very dry.'

'Just dry will do.'

Where does compulsion start, he was thinking. With Pam it had started as a gut reaction. He would have been happy if he hadn't come across some half-finished baby clothes. Too shaken to confront her with the discovery, he had watched

41

like a hawk. But a hawk watches for its dinner; he was watching for his lifestyle.

When she didn't change shape and didn't finish the baby clothes, he realised he was in a situation which could persist as long as their generative powers lasted. He had always thought they shared the same fears and expectations. They had muddled along in ignorance and bliss. Now he saw what could be coming to them, and she wanting it to come, knitting for it. The very idea of birth was abhorrent. A clumsy, squalid, risky business. Pollenation had it beat every time. He wanted none of it for Pam – or himself.

As he set the sherry before her, she said, 'Why is this pub called the "Dolly Pentreath"? Did she die of drink?'

'Look,' he said, 'we're here on holiday in a lovely place, the Cornish riviera, we're supposed to enjoy ourselves.'

'It's me, isn't it? It must be me not enjoying this lovely place.'

'Is it because you're pregnant?' She looked up, startled. 'Because if you are—'

'I'm not, of course I'm not! It's nothing to do with that—'

'It's got to be doing with something.'

'I hoped it didn't show.'

'By God, Pam, you'd better tell me the truth.'

'I've told you the truth. Why on earth should you think otherwise?'

'Because you're making baby clothes.'

She stared, the penny dropped, light dawned and she laughed. 'Those! They're dolls' clothes!'

'Where's the doll?'

'My landlady – she used to be my landlady – her little girl was always dragging her doll around stark naked. I couldn't bear to see it. I promised to make it an outfit so it would look like a real baby and she'd get the idea and be gentle with it.'

He said, 'You're really sticky, you know that?'

She sighed. 'This lovely place worries me. The loveliness doesn't go deep.'

'What's that supposed to mean?'

'Don't be angry, please Nanty. Sometimes I don't even think about it. Yesterday I was lying on the beach watching the gulls hovering and soaring and I thought this will put me right. It's what I've been waiting for.'

Exasperated, he sank half his pint in one swallow. 'Gulls are what it takes to put you right?'

'Then I saw a huge great face, up on the cliff, leering at me.'

'Oh come on, if you're on the beach and there's a man on the cliff you wouldn't be able to see him leer.'

'There wasn't a man, only a face, hundreds of feet of face in the rock, like those American presidents.'

'You dreamed it.'

'Dreams reveal what you're thinking.'

'It was a trick of the light on a geological formation.' She sipped her sherry and grimaced. He said, 'I can see you're not going to enjoy this holiday. You've made up your mind not to.'

'I feel as if something's waiting to happen.'

'Why did you come?'

'To be with you.'

He might have told her she was going the wrong way about it. He might have told her a thing or two. He twiddled his empty glass. 'I think I'll have another.'

At the bar counter someone was holding forth. 'I've nothing against the English weekend. It's an institution, but only for the Establishment. Essential services should maintain their essence through Monday to Monday. The veriest banger has the right to have its wants supplied on a Saturday afternoon. My car's a very banger, it's sitting in the road like a broody hen and you tell me no one will do anything about it.'

'You might find a garage open for repairs in Falmouth,' said the barmaid.

'How do I get to Falmouth?'

'There's a bus tomorrow afternoon.'

He winked at her. 'What'll I do till then?'

He was pleasantly pissed, thought Antony, envying the condition.

'There's a hotel.' The barmaid drew Antony's second pint. 'The Bellechasse. This gentleman's staying there.'

'The Bellwhat?'

'It's French for nice hunting,' said Antony.

'Sounds expensive.'

'It's not.'

'Is it far?'

'You could walk it.'

When Antony went back with his beer, Pam said, 'Do you have to keep drinking?'

'Yes.'

'Who was that you were talking to?'

'His car's broken down and he's stranded. He was asking me about the hotel.'

'Our hotel?'

'There's another?'

Pam sighed. 'Drink makes you surly.' It was spoken softly and reasonably but there was no reason.

'Do you know about cars?' The stranded man had come with his go-lucky air and a tot of whisky.

Antony shrugged. 'Not much.'

'There's not much wrong with mine. She's got a charge like a rhino when she's roused. Trouble is rousing her.'

Pam said, 'Don't you belong to any of the motoring organisations?'

'Can't run to it. I'm an underemployed painter.'

'Where did you break down?' asked Antony.

'A mile or so back. Just petered out. The starter motor works but that's all. Probably a screw loose somewhere. You wouldn't take a look, would you?'

'I'll look but I can't promise anything.'

He held out his hand. 'Olssen, Charlie.'

'My name's Wallington, and this is Pam.'

'Would you mind if we go and look at the car?' Olssen said to her.

'I shan't come.'

'We won't be long. Ten minutes there, ten minutes back, two ticks to fix it.'

'I'll go back to the hotel.'

When he and Antony were outside, Olssen said, 'Does she mind?'

'She doesn't like pubs.' Antony had seen a crust of paint on the seat of Olssen's jeans. 'I suppose the bottom's out of the building trade?'

'I guess so.' Olssen sounded unconcerned.

'It's bound to recover. People have to have houses, they don't have to have flowers.'

'Nor pictures.'

'I'm a florist.'

'People have to have flowers for weddings and funerals and to take to hospitals,' Olssen pointed out.

'I picked a bunch from the hedgerow, to see how many varieties there were. I counted forty-five.'

'Mostly weeds?'

'They were flowers, beautiful and free-gratis.'

'What did you do with them?'

'Threw them away. Pam didn't want them. She said, like you, they were weeds.'

Olssen was starting to roll. Antony liked him for it, he didn't trust a man with a strong head. They came to a bend in the road. Olssen pointed with an unsteady finger, 'There she is.' With the bonnet up, the car looked ready to take a bite. 'Going like the clappers till we got here. She knew I was thinking of taking her to the breakers.'

'If it's a simple fault and I can spot it I might be able to get you going.'

Antony tried the starter. It whirred but did not fire the engine. 'Can you rely on the petrol gauge?'

'I took on ten litres at Truro, it was working then.'

'Seems the petrol's not getting through. I'll check the fuel pump. Have you got a rag?'

Charlie rooted in a holdall on the back seat and brought out a piece of material. Antony held it ready while he disconnected the fuel pipe. A few drops of petrol spilled out. 'Turn on the ignition.' Olssen obeyed and petrol squirted on to the cloth. 'Pump's okay.' Antony reconnected the pipe. 'These yours?' He held up the petrol-soaked cloth – a pair of silk pants.

'Hell, no.'

'You've got some hairy old plugs. When were they last changed?'

'Not in my lifetime.'

'I'd say it's either a problem within the carburettor or an ignition fault. The plugs need sandblasting, or better still, renewing. I'm not an expert, you don't have to take my word.'

'I'll take it. What do I do now?'

'Wait till Monday.' Antony wiped his hands on the briefs.

'Those must be Lumsden's. I'd forgotten his pack on the back seat.'

'There's someone with you?'

'He missed the bus. What's it like where you're staying?'

Ernie Clapham was sitting with his feet in the goldfish pond, as was his custom on warm evenings. Pam thought it disgusting. Imagining the softness and coolness of the water, Antony was tempted to take off his shoes and socks

47

and dip in, but the thought of intruding on another man's solitary pleasure inhibited him.

Clapham looked up as Antony and Olssen approached. 'Nothing to beat a paddle when you've been on your feet all day.'

'Mr Olssen would like a room,' said Antony.

Clapham splashed and churned up the water. 'The fish tickle my toes, no one's done that since I was a babe in arms.'

'And something to eat,' said Olssen.

'The wife will fix you a sandwich.'

'I haven't eaten since breakfast.'

'There may be some soup left.'

Olssen put his hands on his knees and stooped over the pond. 'Look at those colours – green and white like a spring onion. Water plays the devil with skin tones.'

'Never did mine any harm.' Clapham hauled up his feet. 'I'll show you your room.'

Antony left them climbing the stairs. Pam was in their bedroom, sitting on the bed. She said, 'You've been ages. Why have you been such ages?'

'I couldn't get Olssen's car started.'

'Whose car?'

'Charlie Olssen's the chap we met in the pub. He's booked in here.'

'Did you know Dolly Pentreath was the last woman to speak the old Cornish?'

'Who told you that?'

He hoped she had found someone to talk to, but she said

she had overheard it while she was waiting. 'I've been waiting ages, sitting thinking.'

'Why didn't you go to bed?'

'I wouldn't sleep.'

'Take a book, read yourself to sleep.'

'I keep remembering – that man carrying the child – its clothes all wet.'

She was staring at him wide – no, wild-eyed – and he thought, Here we go again. 'Look . . .' Wherever she looked she wouldn't see the crabhold round his heart. 'I'm going down for a bit.'

'Don't go Nanty, stay with me—'

He blundered to the door, making as if he hadn't heard. He wished he hadn't brought Pam here. The place had bad vibes, bringing out the worst in her. Her worst, he thought glumly, might count as the best in some women. Loyalty, devotion, which she undoubtedly had, emerged as clinging, which he had never wanted in a woman. Her whimsies, which had been light-hearted and irresponsible, now threatened to engulf him.

There was no one in what the Claphams called the 'sitter'. The television was showing a picture of its own choosing – a black and white blizzard. Antony switched it off.

Without people, this was still a noisy room. He put it down to the chair covers which were unflaggingly chintz, with Afro-modern spinning suns and some geometric patterns mixed with cottage-garden teenies. There was yet another design of muscular vines with leaves like steaks. He sat to examine it more closely.

It surprised him how some people regarded flowers. Women asked for the 'old jam-tart roses'. 'We spent a fortune decorating the church for when the bishop came,' said a vicar's wife. 'We did roses because they were his favourite flower. But they were those new button things and they never opened out. Of course abroad they use plastic which has to be kept clean. I don't see our ladies sponging the arum lilies as an act of faith.' A man ordering a bouquet had told him, 'The last time I took gypsophila into the house my wife accused me of mental cruelty.' Antony had heard that growers were tidying up the self-destruct factor.

Mildred Gascoigne came in, observing that she was tempted to stroll as far as the field gate. 'The cove looks so pretty when the lights come on.'

'Ah,' said Antony.

'Oh, am I disturbing you?'

'Of course not.'

'Do you know the gate I mean?'

He thought she sounded wistful, and hoped she wouldn't suggest they take a stroll together. Charlie Olssen walked in as he was starting to jingle coins in his pocket. 'Did I just see a Leda and her Swan on a pair of Bermuda shorts?'

'Senga wears a garment with a strange device,' said Mildred.

'Girl nursing a big duck,' supplied Antony.

'Hanging a Leonardo on her butt is blasphemy,' said Charlie.

Gilbert Eashing wrote to his solicitor, who was a personal friend and confidant: 'The last girl you sent came for a day out, she wanted to sunbathe. I was a tertiary consideration if, indeed, I was considered at all. The girl before her believed that age discredits everything, even experience. Especially experience. She was an addicted gossip and would have made my life a buzz.'

He manoeuvred his chair to the threshold of his room. Whenever he wheeled along the passage to the toilet people were wont to ask where he was heading and try to help by pushing. Fortunately, he had a handbrake which he could pull on hard, sometimes winding the pusher. 'I can manage,' he would say, conserving his dignity.

The maid-of-all-work was in the cloakroom, on her knees, washing the floor. She looked up as he hauled his chair through the door.

'I'm supposed to do this before you come in.'

'Don't mind me.'

She wore a sacking apron. He wondered where she had found it: there were no sacking aprons in the shops. She sat on her heels to watch him get out of his chair. He didn't mind her watching. He gripped the jamb of the cubicle door with one hand, the door itself with the other and pulled himself to his feet, swivelling to push the chair clear of the door. As he started to close it she said, 'You've done that before.'

When he came out, she was gone. The floor was under a film of water. He got his slippers wet and swore mildly.

Back in his room, he finished his letter. 'Don't send any more girls, it's a waste paying for their fares and lunches. I must look for a nurse-companion who is strong, well-washed and mute.'

As it was a fine morning he decided to make the trip to the postbox along the lane. Seeing if he could get there by his will-power would be in the nature of a test. He feared deterioration in the strength of his hands and arms.

An unrolled grit track led from the hotel to the road. The wheels of his chair picked up grit which transferred to his palms. He paused to wipe them just as a car turned in at the gate, obliging him to get himself and his chair on to the verge.

The effort made his heart knock on his ribs. That was another thing, cardiac arrest: it was also possible for a lung to collapse under strain, arteries to clog, the nervous system to fail – the body had so many degenerative processes at its disposal.

He was not ready to die. He set the chair in motion, rolled out into the lane, past a board bearing an inscription 'Bellechasse Hotel, props. Mr & Mrs E. Clapham'. It was unlikely to rate a star in the Michelin guide, but it suited him. He had researched extensively before deciding to come here and had reasonable expectations as well as whimsical hopes of names such as Gumpas St. George, Blowhouse Moor, Goonhallow, Trywoos and Butteriss. His interest was in funerary sculpture and there was always the chance of coming across an undocumented joy, a masterstroke among the standard English repertoire.

The lane was full of moving shadows cast by a thicket hedge of big oily leaves. The gradient necessitated a steady haul. He began to tire. Suddenly the shadows seemed to coalesce – the girl he had seen the previous evening in the hotel dining room was beside him.

She said, 'You could get an electric buggy.'

Saving his breath, he hauled himself along, trying to escape her hand which was on the back of his chair.

'There are ones you can turn on a sixpence. If you've got a sixpence.'

'Where would be the advantage?'

'You want to be mobile?'

'Up to a point. Rushing around is no longer necessary. Anyway, I intend to walk again.'

A magpie flew up from the road, almost under his wheels.

'One for sorrow,' said the girl. 'But there's another in the hedge – two for joy.'

The postbox was now only yards away, but she held on to his chair, halting it. 'Do you know Piper?'

'Who?'

'He's staying at the hotel. At least he was. He's gone off somewhere.'

'His car passed me in the drive a few minutes ago.'

'That was him? Piper?'

Eashing said, 'I have not actually made his acquaintance. Be good enough to let me get to the postbox.'

'Sorry.' She gave his chair a vigorous push. He reached up to drop his letter in the box and when he turned she was running back along the lane.

That night, as so often, he dreamed he was running –

beautifully, as a bird flies; and convinced himself that what he most desired was possible, he had only to rise up from his chair and walk.

That ambition should dwindle to the performance of a simple reflex was humiliating. He yearned for the privileged years when he could move about unaided. He watched everyone else exercising the right of passage, their hip-joints rolling easily in a cup of bone, and on the quiet wept tears of impotence and despair.

The Claphams' room being next to his on the ground floor with only a party-wall between, he heard more about their private life than he cared to (though sometimes he kept his hearing-aid in and listened just for company). He learned that Mrs Clapham blamed her husband for their misfortunes. As he was a born loser she might well have faulted his chromosomes, but chose to blame his lubricity.

'She's got to go. Either she goes or I do. I'm not staying under the same roof as her. She's bad luck, nothing's been right since she came. She's put the finger on me.'

'Finger? What finger?'

'Old Scratch's.'

'Edie, you're talking crap.'

'You brought her here to gratify your animal appetite—'

'I brought her here to wait at tables and do the veggies – to help you.'

Eashing wondered how the girl had come by the reputation of a demoniac. He discounted the episode of the flying casserole as evidence of Mrs Clapham's neurosis. The girl herself was little more than a child to whom youth had not been kind. She had acne, was overweight and perpetually open-mouthed. That could be due to adenoids or innocence: an encounter with Clapham's animal appetite would certainly come into the category of experience.

Piper had tried writing detective fiction but could never contrive to hide the identity of his murderer until the last page. Also, he had technical trouble with the actual killing. His corpses were unenterprising and he was told that his clues lacked originality and his narrative style was reminiscent of the old *Quiver* magazine. Investigating that criticism he had discovered possibilities in the agony columns of yester-year. From them he deducted that the *manner* of counselling was more important than the counsel. The sort of people who wrote in, baring their souls, did not want advice, they wanted to be the centre of someone's attention. He managed to convince an editor that involvement and an open mind were all that were needed, and was allotted a regular page under his own logo – a listening ear.

He achieved his success with warm-hearted chats about human dilemmas and how to face up to them. He relied a lot on love, in the home and out of it, thought of himself as a smoother-out of wrinkles in the woof of life and felt no resentment when his advice was ignored. Replying to the *cris de coeur* addressed to him personally was part of his brief. He did not find it a chore.

A package was waiting for him, last week's Listening Ear correspondence, forwarded from the London office, an unusually large bundle of letters, promising to keep him busy.

The telephone rang. It was Sam, breathless over the wire. 'I didn't tell. You said not to and I didn't.'

'What didn't you tell?'

'Where you are.'

'Tell who? Calm down, take a big breath and hold it.'

'She kept saying it was business. Important, she said. I didn't know, I never know with you.'

Piper said, 'My dear, you know exactly.'

'She said she had access and she'd fax you. That bad?'

'Who was this person?'

'A bird.' Sam mourned, 'I'm lonesome. Why don't I come to you?'

'Sam, no. I have to work and there's no one here you'd take to.'

'You don't want me!'

He would be showing the whites of his eyes, between fear and anger, the fear of losing his regular handouts. Piper's own feelings were mixed. He was fond of the boy: Sam's poor look-out worried him. He felt compassion and a certain unease, as if he sighted an ambush. 'Don't be such a goose.' Prudently he rang off.

His thoughts kept reverting to the unknown female seeking to know his whereabouts: the sense of ambush was strong.

He wandered down to the beach, a dog's leg of grey shingle in a rocky cove. Spiky pink flowers clung to the cliff-face. A slick of weed marked high water. Beyond it was an area of mud: streams leaking over it kept it to the consistency of melted cocoa. Bladderwrack, advancing and retreating with the pull of the tide, rolled up a plastic bottle. Piper toed it before him until it was swept out of reach. He saw it brought out and in again, never quite making the land and having no function there anyway. A cabin cruiser, its hull bright with algae, rested comfortably on its side. Gulls, also comfortable, perched on the gunwales.

Piper trod on over the shingle, observing that it was constituted of grit, chips of marble, scoured glass, straw and winkle shells. His feet slithered on kelp. This was not, never would be, a development area: the inlet was so narrow that there was only tunnel vision to the sea. Boats of any size, when they came up at all, had to come single file and hug the rock to pass each other.

But there was a small concrete landing-stage and someone sitting, cross-legged. He looked up as Piper approached, waved two fingers, then bent to the board held across his knees.

Drawing near, Piper saw that he was sketching a tree on the cliff, a skinny sapling lodged in a crevice and clinging in virtual extremis to the rock face. He said, 'See this tree? Its guts are being squeezed dry and it's got nowhere else to grow.' He sketched a penumbra round the tree, intensifying it. 'There's an altar-piece by a German Renaissance painter showing an arm and a leg sticking out from under a stone slab. The unquiet grave. It was done for the chapel of a hospital order and the sick saw it every time they went to pray for a cure.'

'How has that to do with your picture?'

He looked up at Piper. There were smudges of charcoal under his nose. 'This little tree has been buried alive and is trying to escape.'

There were new faces at dinner. Mildred Gascoigne had a friend at her table, which did not stop her greeting Piper. 'How was London?'

'As usual, grey and grubby.'

'I always think it's so colourful.'

'The only colour I saw was in Royal Hospital Road.'

'Hospital? You're not ill – there's nothing wrong?'

Aware that every face was turned his way, he said briefly, 'Chelsea pensioners.'

Unrolling her napkin, Mildred dropped the ring which bowled across the floor directly to Piper's feet. He handed the ring back to her.

She thanked him with effusion and the girl at her table quizzed him openly. A man at the window table put on horn-rims and looked at Piper over the top. The woman with him wore star-spangled spectacles and had a vulpine smartness which chilled. 'Soulsby,' said the man, nodding. 'Felicia,' said the woman, glittering.

Mrs Clapham came, bringing hors d'oeuvres, plates balanced on each arm. Her mouth was tight shut, her nostrils dilated. She dumped the plates on the tables and swept out. When she returned with two more hors d'oeuvres, Pam Wallington asked where Bettony was.

'She tried to kill me.'

Pam cried, 'What?'

Mrs Clapham put the plates on the Soulsbys' table. A blast from her nostrils lifted Mrs Soulsby's fringe. 'She threw a stewpan at me, inch-thick earthenware it was. I saw it coming. I ducked and it went through the kitchen door.'

'Some throw,' said Soulsby.

'The door wasn't open.'

They were a moment taking in the meaning. 'It went *through* the door?' said Pam, incredulous. Mrs Clapham nodded, dignified, even haughty. 'Through the thickness of the door? That's not possible!'

'That is what I mean.' Mrs Clapham went, taking the Soulsbys' wine with her.

Pam looked round at them all. 'What do you make of that?'

'There was still wine in our bottle,' said Soulsby.

'Poor Bettony!' said Mildred Gascoigne.

Clapham, wearing a white jacket, brought the second course. 'The wife's resting. She's had a bit of a turn.'

'What has happened to Bettony?'

'Wife locked her out.'

Pam said, 'Did she really – what Mrs Clapham said?'

'Throw the stewpot? She couldn't, it was on a high shelf, she couldn't reach it down, poor little cow.'

Mrs Soulsby said, 'The girl's pubescent, it sounds as if there's a poltergeist at work.'

'Have you *seen* anything?' said Pam.

'Poltergeists don't show themselves.'

'We saw a fox,' said Soulsby.

'I don't mind the wildlife.'

Pam Wallington said, 'I saw a man carrying a dead child.'

'Cut it out, Pam,' said her husband.

Mrs Soulsby held up a restraining hand. 'You saw what?'

'It was dripping wet. It had been drowned.'

'When was this?'

'Years ago,' Antony said hastily, 'at the seaside. Nobody has been drowned, for God's sake!'

Pam, ready to burst into tears, insisted, 'He was old, the man, his eyes fixed me – like looking into the headlights of a car—'

'Many a rabbit I've caught in my headlights and popped in the pot still warm,' said Clapham.

'When I looked back there was nothing and no one!'

'How very interesting,' said Mrs Soulsby. 'Cornwall is well known for paranormal perceptions. Quite possibly you witnessed a telesthetic event which was happening in another place at that same time or even quite a different moment.'

Antony Wallington said, 'Please don't alarm my wife.'

'I hear trees in the night,' said Mildred Gascoigne. 'Big trees stirring in the wind. Such a sad, wild sound.'

'A woman here once swore she heard wolves.' Clapham grinned. 'Funny though, she was stone deaf. What you hear, Miss Gee, is the tide on the turn.'

'What about Mrs Clapham and the flying casserole,' said Mrs Soulsby. 'How do you account for that?'

'Imagination. I blame the Change.' Clapham gave it a confederate grin and capital letter.

'It wasn't years ago at the seaside,' said Pam. 'It was here, yesterday.'

There was a pause. Nobody moved, except Piper, who walked out.

'Cooee!' Felicia Soulsby called round the kitchen door. 'I haven't come to interrupt, just to see if you're feeling better.'

Mrs Clapham was operating some sort of pulverizer which had to be worked by hand. She looked round with rancour, and the pulverizer gathered momentum. 'It must have been awfully upsetting,' said Felicia.

'What must?'

'That business with the casserole – enough to put anyone off their stride.'

'Nothing wrong with *me*.'

There was a shelf high up, and empty. As Clapham had said, Bettony could not have reached it. Nor could Mrs Clapham, unless she stood on a chair.

Felicia was interested to see that Bettony was back, peeling potatoes. 'Do you think it detracts from the flavour? Washing potatoes before you peel them?'

'I've told her again and again, hold them under the tap first. She can't take it in. She can't take anything in.' Mrs Clapham looked into the pulverizer and stirred the contents with her finger. 'He said she was all he could get. He had his reasons.'

'He?'

'Clapham.' A change came over Mrs Clapham's face. It skewed, as if the wrong string had been pulled. 'He knew

61

he could do what he liked and she'd be backward in coming forward.' Felicia experienced a frisson of distaste but was unsure how deep it ought to go. Mrs Clapham clinched it. 'Men are all the same.'

'Of course it's distracting when anything is misplaced. I get into an absolute tiz if I can't put my hand on what I need when I'm cooking.'

'It wasn't misplaced, it was thrown. By her.' Mrs Clapham aimed her thumb in Bettony's direction.

'It may have been done on her behalf, though not actually *by* her.'

'Wasn't nobody else in the room.'

'I'm talking about a manifestation.'

'There's none of that in my kitchen.'

'You wouldn't see it but you'd feel the effects. You'd certainly feel those. A teenager undergoing a physical disturbance—'

'Disturbance? Her?' Mrs Clapham said bitterly. 'She's a pudding.'

Cradling a potato to her bosom, Bettony gouged out its eye.

Clapham was not a native of Cornwall. As a young boy he had spent an auspicious holiday there: according to his parents had been allowed to 'run wild'.

Ernie was never one to run wild. He roved, there was nothing else to do. The countryside bored him. While roving, his habit was to slash grasses and flowers with a stick from the hedgerow, aim stones at anything that moved and at every empty bottle on the beach until he smashed it.

In this desultory frame of mind he had got as far as the old house down by the creek. The quality of its disrepair intrigued him. The guttering hung awry, the roof tiles bulged like a bedspread, the paintwork was a grim memory. The place looked as if clouting winds from the sea had knocked it off its perch. It was wacky. Ernie got into the garden and amused himself sparring with shoulder-high nettles, felling them with right hooks and left uppercuts. Not looking where he was going, he had a shock when he bumped into a woman in a hammock.

Her eyes were closed; she wasn't breathing. He plucked a grass stalk and held it under her nose. It didn't move. She was dead.

She said, not opening her eyes, 'What are you doing here?'

Undismayed – he had heard of chickens running about with their heads cut off – he said, 'Nothing.'

'Who are you?'

'Ernie Clapham.'

'As in the junction?' He fiddled with the grass stalk, waiting. She said, 'You're trespassing.' That was how he met Miss Pendennis, who was to settle his way of life for him. 'I could prosecute you.' She was already old, sitting up in the hammock with a stock of grey hair and yellow eyes like a tiger's.

He turned and ran. She called after him, 'Come back tomorrow and we'll talk about it.'

They never did talk about it, though Ernie went back next day and the next and many days after. There was nothing else to do. She had been a schoolteacher, he could just see her chalking on the blackboard. In the village they resented her living in a big house, setting herself up as a fine lady. People said she had plenty of money but she dispensed no charity, allowed her property to go to rack and ruin, made no friends and few contacts. Ernie came up against hard feelings if he mentioned her. It was easier to keep quiet. He didn't himself know what to make of her.

When she started calling him Ernest, he said, 'Don't call me that.'

'Why not?'

'It's cissy.'

'If it was good enough for Hemingway it's good enough for you.'

Perhaps there *was* something toffee-nosed about her, but he liked talking to her, he was beginning to find his voice and was agreeably surprised by the strength and variety of his convictions. She came alive listening to him airing them. Her eyes weren't yellow, they were sort of amber and glowed when she laughed. She didn't laugh at him, he wouldn't have stood for that; he was able to join in, even when the laugh was on himself.

She never asked him into the house, she watched from the window and came to him in the garden. One day she said, 'How do you get into the garden?'

'Over the wall.'

'But it's so high.'

'I climb into the tree and drop down.'

'Tree? What tree?'

'The big oak that hangs over the wall.'

'I'd rather you didn't.'

'Why?'

'You must stop climbing that tree!'

'I shan't hurt it.'

'*Hurt* it? Oh my God!' She rocked, laughing; it was one time he couldn't join in.

He said stoutly, 'What's up then? It's only an old tree.'

'There's a gate in the wall. I'll give you the key and you can come in that way.'

'I like climbing in. No problem.'

'I want you to promise never to get into that tree again.'

'Oh sure.'

'On your word of honour. If you have one.'

Ernie drew a finger across his neck. After that he made a point of looking closely at the tree. There was nothing to see – no more, anyway, than was to be expected: leaves and branches and a hole in the trunk where owls or something lived. She probably thought he would fall. He would show her what a climber he was. Meantime he accepted the key and used the door. There was a name painted on it – 'Bellechasse'. He asked her what it meant. She said it was French for good hunting.

One day he came and found her lying in the hammock. It was the middle of a heatwave, the hottest day of the year. 'The wireless says there's a storm coming.' She had her eyes shut, like the first time he saw her. But now the fine lines in her face had drawn together, making it a mask. She looked a million years old. Ernie felt a twinge of disquiet. He said, 'Storm makes the wireless crackle. Atmospherics.'

One of her hands was draped out of the hammock and something she had been holding fell to the ground. Ernie picked up a small leather-covered book.

'Give that to me!' Suddenly she was wide awake.

'What is it?'

He was actually handing it over when she pushed it back into his hand. 'Let's see what you can make of it.' The way she spoke, taunting, put his back up.

The book had a bitter smell. He opened it on pages dog-eared and brown at the edges, covered with spidery writing. The words were foreign, nightmarish. Every few pages carried a heading, he guessed it was the date. On some were diagrams and rows of numbers.

'Well? What do you suppose it is?'

'Could be a diary.'

'That's clever of you.' She took the book from him, clasped it prayerwise between her palms. 'It's the diary of a fighter pilot during the Second World War, a day-to-day record of his missions.'

Ernie said alertly, 'You talking about Douglas Bader?'

'This man was German, a Nazi. He doesn't identify himself because that might have given away information to his enemies. I call him Koenig. He was awarded the Iron Cross First Class.'

'Pull the other one.'

'Are you saying you don't believe me?'

66

Ernie was seldom troubled by any sense of unreality. But he felt it now, knew he ought to be dreaming and wasn't. He called her bluff. 'Okay, so read me some of it.' She stared at him, very much the schoolteacher, he the biggest bonehead in her class. 'Where would you get a Nazi's diary, anyway? It's a spoof, someone's having you on.'

'Who?'

'Whoever gave it to you.'

'No one gave it to me.'

'Okay, so what's in it?'

She opened the book. 'This is the entry for two consecutive days in September, 1940: "We carried out intensive raids on London as directed by Reichmarshal Goering—"'

'It's not even in German!'

'I am translating for your benefit: *This was saturation bombing. Our planes, "the choir of vengeance", went over in relays, dropping their bombs at the rate of 25 a minute. The East End took the brunt, the docks were set alight and fires lit up the sky. I could feel – many of us pilots did – the repercussion of the heavy calibre bombs from three miles up.*'

She put the book down and stared at Ernie. He said, 'I'm thirsty.' She rose without a word and went into the house. He picked up the book, thumbed over the pages and came on a crude drawing of a woman with a dog's head cradling a machine gun in her arms. When Miss Pendennis returned, bringing a glass of water, he thrust the book at her. 'What's this?'

'The wolf-headed goddess of the dead. The words underneath are "Goddess strikes England".'

'Daft!' Ernie made off, not waiting to drink the water.

The storm came and went, the heat stayed. He went every day to hear her read. Years later, looking back on that time, it was the heat he remembered, the weight of it, clouds reaching into the sky, solids melting and merging. And the company of Koenig. He had got a picture of him without knowing how. The funny thing was – and a bit sickening – the picture of a man in grey uniform with an iron cross round his neck kept leaking into his picture of Miss Pendennis, grey-faced, in rusty black, wearing a torn hairnet. She watched him from under her shaggy brows as she read, twitching the pages as if impatient to get to the end.

Ernie liked best the descriptions of mid-air battles, the dogfights. Each day, when he was alone, he took up where the previous reading had left off. His wanderings ceased to be aimless, now he was scouring the skies for the enemy. He was flying a Messerschmitt-jet with the wolf-headed woman, the goddess of death, painted on his fuselage. He didn't think much about her, except that it might be as well to have her along. Spreading his arms, he plunged into the long grass, uttering his own lifelike imitation of an engine on full throttle, dodged attacks from heads of cow-parsley, swerved to take avoiding action from bursts of flak from anti-aircraft batteries in haystacks, shot up pylons, circled church spires and skimmed telegraph wires in the best tradition of aerial combat.

A Hurricane dived at me out of the sun. I dodged and as soon as I had him in my gun-sight I closed in, gave him a burst

*dead on target. He whipped round, trying to come underneath
me. I let him have another salvo. He did a half roll and got
through a hole in the cloud. I went after him and attacked
from close quarters, close enough to see my bullets rip into his
wings and the slipstream to peel bits off. He started to spin
down, recovered and zoomed vertically. I pressed the trigger
again. He lost his rudder, one of his wings came off. The plane
stalled and nosedived. The pilot dropped out, his parachute
opened, the last I saw he was hanging in the harness like a
broken doll.*

She said, 'What do you make of it?'

'Great stuff, better than *The Boys' Own Paper*.'

'Stuff? This is real, this is how it was, death and wanton destruction!' He nodded. She said bitterly, 'It must be
an occasion for applause when the destroyers turn on the
instruments of destruction as in this daylight raid on an
airfield: *It was entre-nous, so to speak and we were looking
forward to a bit of our own back. Our orders were to attack
from an ultra-low level. Navigation was easy. After crossing
the Channel we followed the railway line inland. As we roared
over, passengers on the station platforms dispersed like tealeaves
under a jet of water. Shooting up people in the streets is something
some of my co-pilots indulge in. I prefer to reserve my bullets for
dogfights. With the quarry in my gun-sight and my thumb on the
gunbutton a Spitfire is my intended, I go after it like a lover.*

*There was no interception that morning. Halifaxes and
Blenheims rested peacefully on the grass, someone's weekend toy,
a little biplane painted in rainbow colours, nestling alongside. I*

thought they should have put that out of sight. I also spotted a pair of longjohns staked out to dry. Then our bombers emerged from cloud cover and the raid was on. Bombs bounded down the runway, hangars collapsed in a sea of flame which went leaping up to the sky. The ground swarmed with running men. We picked off their machines one by one. A few struggled up, finding spaces between the bombs. I shot down two before they were airborne and sent another in a picture-book spiral into a herd of cows.

'Have you kept your word?' she said, snapping the book shut.

'What word?'

'You promised not to climb the oak tree.'

'I promised and I haven't,' he said sulkily.

'That's somewhat equivocal. Could you please be more precise?'

'I wouldn't climb your rotten old tree if it was the last rotten old tree in the world!'

She sighed. 'These aren't bedtime stories I'm reading.'

Ernie couldn't see the connection – if there was any, it was an insult. He said, 'I'm going home tomorrow,' as if it was his own decision. In fact, the letter from his parents had come as an unwelcome surprise. Not only did he not want to go home at this juncture, the idea dismayed him. He would have to go sometime, but the time was not yet. He wasn't finished here.

Miss Pendennis was surprised too. The grey went out of her face: she turned sort of off-white. 'So soon?'

As Ernie saw it, there were several possible answers to that: like 'all good things come to an end', or 'there's nothing to keep me here'. He decided it was more important to seem not to care less. 'My parents will be picking me up around noon.' He brushed grass seeds off his trousers. 'Pity about the reading.'

'There's one more passage I'd like you to hear.'

This time she did not watch him as she read, kept her head lowered over the page. *'Based on the Pas de Calais, our orders were to make several sorties a day, to and fro across the Straits of Dover. I took my briefing from the flaxen Gretchen of a boy with dimpled wrists, the blithe spirit of HQ and something of a little god: "Assemble at altitude 18,000, prepare to climb to 30,000 over the English coast." I said, "That's the lower limit of the stratosphere." He laughed in my face. "You'll need it, they're waiting for you." I could have killed him, not from anger, from the longing to feel my hands on his pretty neck.'*

'Damn cold up there, nought centigrade,' Ernie said. 'We did the stratosphere at school in General Science.'

'I presume you asked to go home?'

Miffed, he said, 'Of course I didn't,' and realised, too late, that it was an admission of parental control. 'I'm not bothered one way or the other.'

If she believed him, she didn't show it. 'I don't expect I'll see you again.'

'Reckon I'll be busy packing tomorrow morning.'

'Goodbye, Ernie.' She held out her hand.

He gave her the key of the garden door. 'You can lock up behind me. But watch out someone else doesn't climb in through the tree.'

He was halfway across the garden when she said, 'That's

71

where he died.' Ernie turned to find her close behind him. 'Koenig,' she said, 'in that tree.'

'What?'

'He was shot down, his parachute caught in the branches. He hung there three days and nights, he couldn't free himself, both his arms were broken. I think he must have had internal injuries as well, he bled so much. He cried, every time I went to him he cried, pleading, like a child to its mother.'

Ernie couldn't speak. He told himself, You don't speak when you're dreaming, when you have a nightmare your tongue's tied.

She said, 'I didn't tell anybody he was there. The beach was mined and the creek fenced off with barbed wire, so no one came this way. I left him to die. After the atrocities he and his kind committed should I have had pity? I hardened my heart, my heart was like a stone. And then we bombed Dresden, thousands of women and children were slaughtered and that beautiful city was razed to the ground. I thought enough is enough, one more is too much, and I went out to him. It was too late, he had strangled in the cords of his parachute.'

The sun beating down made Ernie feel sick. He couldn't make it to the shade of the oak tree.

She said, 'After he was gone, I picked up the diary which had fallen from his pocket. When at last they found him I pretended I hadn't known he was there. They accepted that. But I don't want you in that tree ever again.' With her finger she lifted a bead of sweat from his cheek. 'The evil those men did lives on in all of us. Even in you, blameless child.'

When she died she left the house in trust to Ernie. He did not change the name; he rather fancied 'Bayview', but 'Bellechasse' was classier for a hotel.

Elissa said she'd asked her neighbours to tea.

'Why?'

'Why not?'

Owen shrugged. He had mixed reactions: for a man in his position the mixture was unethical. When Elissa said, 'I'd like to know her better,' he was tempted to ask why again. She said, 'Shall I make a chocolate fudge cake for the boy?'

Seeing her and Angela Hartop in close proximity with each other was disorientating. Angela had dressed for an occasion, though, as Elissa remarked later, it was scarcely a teatime one. She wore a black dress with chunky gold jewellery at neck and wrists. Her hair, pulled up through a bandeau, spilled over in fiery ringlets. Elissa, as familiar to him as his own self, lost her place in his world. It was temporary, but for an unappreciable time he seemed not to have a world at all. It took several cups of tea to restore it.

'Where's James?' said Elissa.

'Watching television.'

'I made a cake for him.'

'I never could cook. Greville used to say my custard was a killer.'

'Shall I cut you a piece? Then you might like to take the rest of it back to James.'

'How kind you are.' She ate her cake with enjoyment, accepted another slice and pinched up the crumbs. 'Isn't it really weird – this will turn into me but the rest will turn into James.'

'Does he mind being left?' was the nearest Elissa could get to a reprimand.

'He doesn't take after his father.' Angela seemed to think that was answer enough. 'I loved my husband.' Owen thought he detected a note of challenge. 'We were so happy, the three of us. Greville was always bringing presents for James and me, it was his delight to surprise us. James has a cupboard full of toys his father bought him. I can't bear to see him playing with them, I've locked them away. Greville brought me jewellery. I remember how he loved to deck me in it. I can't wear any of it now. I buried it.'

'But you dug it up again?' said Elissa.

'This is costume stuff.' Angela fingered her necklace. 'Greville gave me real gold and diamonds.'

Owen said 'Ah', which was safe, even with feeling. The feeling was real, but what was it a feeling *of*?

'Him dying was so sudden. I thought he was asleep. He looked lovely, so peaceful, I didn't like to disturb him. I covered him with a rug and went to bed. In the morning he was stone cold.'

Owen thought, Is this right? Should she share the saddest moments of her life with virtual strangers?

Elissa said afterwards it wasn't what she'd heard. 'By all accounts it was a far from happy marriage. They fought like cat and dog, went at it something dreadful.'

'Judging by the terminology,' Owen said, 'the accounts are Mrs Latimer's.'

Elissa gathered up the tea things. 'She forgot to take James's cake.'

Owen had formed a habit of walking to the village shop after breakfast to buy a newspaper. Along the lane he came upon James sitting cross-legged in the road.

'What's this? What are you doing?'

'Sitting.'

'I can see that. Why?'

'I'm tired.'

'Don't you know it's risky sitting in the middle of the road?'

'I have to go to the police station.'

'For Pete's sake!'

'Who's Pete?'

'Why are you going to the police station?'

'The policeman thinks you drowned me.'

'Who told you that?'

'She said I said so. She was angry.'

'Your mother?'

'Did I? I didn't mean to. I have to stop him coming to arrest you.'

Owen laughed. 'Nobody's going to arrest me. We're in the clear, you and I.'

'Is Pete your son?'

Owen took one look at his darkening face and lifted him to his feet. 'Tell you what, let's go to the shop and buy sweets for you and a newspaper for me.'

'Is he?' Tight-lipped, James pulled at Owen's hand.

Owen ruffled his hair. 'I have no son, old son.'

James's face cleared. He touched his cheek on Owen's hand and ran ahead along the lane.

The woman in the village store – a collateral, surely, of Mrs Latimer – spoke in breathy whispers while James was choosing his sweets. She obviously believed he could not hear her. 'Him and his father were real pals. They used to come and buy chocolate and Coke, sherbet and liquorice allsorts, he didn't need to look twice at anything he fancied. But once the father was gone, the poor lamb was never let near. She said he was losing his teeth through too much sweet stuff. I told her, they're milk teeth, he's going to lose them anyway. This is the first I've seen him since Mr Hartop went. He loved to come here, laughing and larking with the boy. I said to my husband I've seen that man lose himself in the one bit of happiness he's likely to have—'

'What are milk teeth?' James had come to the counter.

'My, my!' Halted in full flood, the woman leaned over to look at him. 'Little pitchers have big ears. I was talking to this gentleman about things you couldn't understand.'

'I understand everything!'

'My, my.' She winked at Owen. 'Little Master Knowall! We should put him on the telly—'

'Why don't you bloody shut up!' Glaring, James tore open a packet and shook out the contents. Red, green and yellow sweets bounced and rolled across the floor. He trod on them as he made for the door. The shopkeeper cried out. Owen said, 'Oh lord! I'm sorry – I'll come back and settle with you,' and ran after James.

He caught up with him in the lane, spoke with more mildness than he felt. 'That wasn't nice. Where did you learn such language –' James responded with a look between pride and cunning – 'it's not clever, it's not smart.' Owen lengthened his stride, put distance between the boy and himself. He heard hurrying feet: James was at his heels, whimpering and clinging to the hem of his jacket. Owen rounded on him. 'I don't care where you heard it or who from, it's bad language, and coming from someone your age it's disgusting.'

'Are you angry? Please don't be angry with me—'

'Promise you'll never use such words again.' A tall order to be carried into manhood.

James cried, 'I promise – cross my heart and hope to die!'

Owen told Angela, 'I found him sitting in the middle of the road.'

She was opening a box of cornflakes and did not look up. 'He was probably waiting for you.'

'I think you should know.'

'Of course.'

'He's out there now, swinging on the gate.' Owen said sharply, 'I'm fond of him and he seems to like being with me, but he can't always be.'

'I didn't know he'd gone out. It shan't happen again.'

'Can you guarantee it? I'd hate to feel in any way to blame if something happened.'

She looked up. 'Will you come back later – this evening, after he's in bed? I must talk to you.'

She was holding the box of cornflakes in her arms – 'A great British Breakfast, fortified with 9 added vitamins'.

Owen resisted the urge to touch her hair.

'Talk? What about?' said Elissa.

'James, if I'm not mistaken.'

'Do you want to get involved?'

'I think she's having trouble with him.'

'Nothing, surely, that can't be sorted out at school.'

'I asked why he doesn't go to school.'

'What did she say?'

'She didn't.' An equivocation, Owen knew: he had asked the boy, not his mother.

'Mrs Latimer says they wouldn't accept him for play-school because he vandalised the toy cupboard.'

'It figures.' Owen grinned. 'He's knocked the stuffing out of his woolly rabbit.'

'He would, wouldn't he – she's kept him from the toys his father bought him. The trouble,' Elissa said crisply, 'will be of her making.'

She had taken against Angela Hartop, thanks to the invidious Mrs Latimer. 'A woman either loves or hates, there is no middle course'. Horace probably said that.

Angela was at the window, watching. Owen didn't altogether relish being watched for.

'I was afraid you wouldn't come.'

It seemed that the answer to Elissa's question was that he was already involved. 'Is James in bed?'

'Yes, but he's being tiresome and won't settle. Let's go where he can't hear us.'

Owen followed her into a small room stocked rather than furnished with an over-large suite, a break-front cabinet and a pottery Alsatian. There was a disused air, like that of the front parlours of his youth.

'Do sit down. It's called "The Tree of Heaven".'

'Sorry?'

'The design.' She patted the settee beside her.

'What did you want to talk about?'

'I want you to know the truth.'

'About James?'

'It's more than that' – she was impatient – 'much more—'

He held out his hand: she took it, came to her knees at his side. This time he did not resist: he touched her hair, threaded it through his fingers, as soft and silken as he had known it would be. But when she turned his hand and kissed his palm, he stood up, pulling her to her feet. Confused by his own feelings, he was unprepared for hers. She put her arms round his waist and folded against him. He didn't believe it was happening, but didn't Horace say 'the story is about you'?

It was the child who reminded him that he was about to commit adultery: James, in his pyjamas, holding the rabbit-thing by its remaining ear. 'He can't sleep.'

'Why not?'

'Because he can't shut his eyes!'

'Poor fellow,' said Owen.

'Come and read to me.'

79

Angela said, 'Back to bed with you at once!'

Owen glimpsed James's expression of open malice, fleeting and not unnatural in a child reproved.

'Tell you what, we'll read till you drop off. I know what it's like when you can't sleep.' He whispered to Angela, 'I'll be back.'

When James was in bed, there was the question of what to read.

Owen suggested *Red Riding Hood, Cinderella, Beauty and the Beast*. James pushed the rabbit-thing under the bed-clothes. 'We don't like baby stuff.'

'What do you like?'

James hooted.

Owen told Angela, 'I suppose it was fuddy-duddy suggesting the old fairy-tales, but I think modern kids miss some-thing.'

'Did he go to sleep?'

'Sound. You know – I ought to be going. Elissa frets.'

'Please – stay – hear me out. I haven't been able to tell anyone, but I want you to know. I lied about Greville. He isn't dead.'

'What?'

'I can't take any more . . .' She was breathless, wanting him to know.

Owen said, 'Start at the beginning. Why did you lie?'

'Because – it's not an easy story to tell. Greville's older than me, a lot older. Marrying late in life – we were happy at first, he enjoyed spoiling me, he said it would always be just the two of us, we didn't need anyone else. He didn't want a child, but when James was born he didn't want anything else. He was bewitched by the baby, idolised it, fussed and panicked, fought me over every detail of its care. I felt like an enemy – of my own child.'

'Very distressing.'

'It was ludicrous. As James grew older, Greville tried to grow younger. He tries to play with James – boisterous games – he puts on an old fur coat and pretends to be a bear, chases James all over the house. James doesn't like it.'

Owen said dryly, 'I imagine not.'

'He doesn't realise what an effort his father is making – James despises him, soon gets bored and starts teasing, mocking. It makes me cry. Can you understand? I'm ashamed of my husband – a good, kind sober man, lowering himself to please a child – he's swamped my love for James – I begin to hate James, I can't watch when Greville tries to romp with him.'

Owen, who was wondering where this was leading, said, 'What's Greville's line of business?'

'He's a journalist. He works for a magazine based in London, but he spends a lot of time here, writing. He won't talk about it. When I asked was he writing a novel he said who needs fiction with the sort of truth we're up against?'

'A sobering thought.'

'We quarrelled, we often did, about James, and it was making him moody and withdrawn. Greville wanted to take him away. I told him James was in danger of having a mental breakdown and Greville agreed to go away himself for a while. He didn't go far, he's put up at a hotel just beyond the village. That's where he heard a story about a drowned child – he came rushing back yesterday evening.'

'What happened?'

'It was James he came to see. He wanted to touch him, hold him, to make sure he hadn't been harmed. But James wouldn't stand still, he ran rings around Greville. Trying to catch him, Greville tripped and fell. James dislikes seeing his father look silly – Greville doesn't realise it's the loss of his dignity – I can't help him – he asked about you – cross-examined me.'

'What did you tell him?'

'That you were our new neighbour and kind enough to take James for walks. He was very upset, I could see he didn't think I was telling him the whole story. I had to be so careful, I daren't let him suspect how fond of you James is.'

'I'm sorry,' said Owen. 'It hasn't worked out. I'd better keep away. We must think of something to put James off.'

'No! That's not the answer – I must see you – you're my only breath of sanity – please don't leave me!'

She came uninvited into his arms, raised her face to his. When they kissed, every fibre of his being rejoiced.

Coming off the beach, Charlie found himself face to face with the girl from the roadside café. She greeted him, 'It *is* you, I wasn't sure. I thought you'd grown a moustache.'

Charlie rubbed his upper lip. 'I've never had a moustache.'

'You've been sketching. May I see?'

'It's not finished.'

'Tony Wallington says you're a painter and decorator.'

'Depends what you call decoration.'

'I saw you talking to Piper. Will you introduce me?'

'I don't know your name.'

'It's Senga. Agnes backwards.' She smiled a crooked smile. 'Agnes means chaste.'

Charlie held out his hand. 'Olssen, Charlie. Glad to know you.'

'What were you talking to Piper about?'

'A tree.' When Charlie turned into the lane she followed him.

'Where are you going?'

'To fetch my toothbrush.'

'What sort of thing do you sketch?' She fell into step beside him.

'Every sort of thing.'

'I've got a Samuel Palmer. It's called *Early Morning*. A rabbit is going home, dead tired, been out all night. The trees are like big mushrooms. It's dated 1825.'

'That's one of his Shoreham drawings, rarer than a dealer's tears.'

'It's only a print – fubsy, fubsier than he intended. There's a couple getting up out of a hole in the ground. They've been there all night too. I've hung it in the loo where I have time to look at it. It's the sort of picture I like.'

'What about Leonardo?' Charlie pointed to her shorts.

'Oxfam.' She said, 'Will there be anywhere open to buy a toothbrush?'

'No problem, it's in my car.'

She held up an apple. 'Share with me, I can't eat alone.' Twisting the apple in her hands she broke it neatly in half.

'Where did you learn to do that?'

'Just one of my tricks.'

He believed it. 'My car broke down. I had to leave it and put up at the hotel. It's sheer coincidence you being there.'

'I didn't think it was anything else.'

'You did. In the Hungry Eater.'

'Where?'

'On the A31 beyond Farnham you thought I was following you.'

Charlie lengthened his stride and reached the car just as rain started, heavy meaningful drops like the ones he had left in NW3. She said, 'I'll get in the back.'

'I can't move this car.'

'Out of the rain, Charlie!'

When he got into the driver's seat he noticed, as never before, the build-up of crud in the air-vents and crevices of the dash. Rain splashing through gear and brake outlets had soaked the floorboards. The car seemed to be blaming him for the way it was. 'There's nothing worse than a car that won't go.'

'Change it.'

'Can't afford to. I'm skint.'

Rummaging for his toothbrush which he seemed to remember shoving into the map pocket at the last moment, he disinterred a letter from Nina. 'If you can get that old heap of yours down here I'd love to see you.' She'd love to, but J.T. Crawford wouldn't. Charlie understood that. The letter was dated six months previous and he had not come until obliged by circumstance – lack of ready cash – and a not yet defunct wish to see Nina again.

'You should never deride a machine, it will always get back to you.' He pulled out the choke and turned on the ignition. A whirring, like clockwork running down, then silence.

'Don't your pictures sell?'

'People don't believe in paying for a work of art unless there's no one to take the money except a dealer who picked it up in a job lot and is asking four figures for it at Christie's.' Charlie said glumly, 'I had to part with the best thing I ever did for peanuts.'

She leaned on the back of his seat: her breath tickled his neck. 'I wish I could see it.'

'You might, I'll leave it to the nation.'

'People like you, artists, creators, never die.'

'We die like flies.' Turning, he looked into her yellow-flecked eyes.

'What's this?' She pulled out one of the canvases from Lumsden's pack on the back seat. 'What's it about? Everything's out of proportion!'

'That's the general idea.'

'There's someone watching us – from behind the hedge . . .'

A man climbed over the field gate. Charlie said, 'It's Piper,' and wound down the window. 'Come and take shelter!'

Piper came to the car and looked in. He said, 'I like walking in the rain,' and walked away.

Senga got out and followed him. She caught him up and held Lumsden's canvas over both their heads to keep off the rain.

Drenching mist came in from the sea. Charlie, when he started walking back to the hotel, was made aware of a stealthy withdrawal of solids. From his waist down he was invisible to himself. And had forgotten his toothbrush.

His jacket smelled of wet dog and had let rain through to his wallet. He counted the few limp notes. He had been a fool to take Crawford's cheque, he should have insisted on a fairer price. But if he had, he might have ended with nothing. The cheque would not cover his bed and board at the hotel, much less the repairs to the car – expenses he hadn't reckoned on. He was overdrawn and had had crisp warnings from the bank about continuing to use his credit card. He decided to skip dinner and took an umbrella from the hall-stand.

Senga called from the stairs, 'You're not going out again? It's pissing down.'

'I'm going to the Dolly P.' When he opened the door the wind dealt a backhander which lifted the pictures off the walls.

'Wait.' Senga slipped past him and vanished into the dark. When he tried to put up the umbrella, it thrashed about like a bird in the claws of a cat.

Senga brought her car round, a vintage Morris Minor with

rococo fenders. It had to be forty years old if it was a day. Sie leaned across to open the door.

'Nice,' said Charlie, 'collectable.'

The wind had shredded the mist and was chasing scraps of it in catchment areas. Senga sang as she drove, a song about never seeing a poem lovelier than a tree. Charlie didn't care for the concept.

The sign of the Dolly Pentreath was swinging to and fro. Dolly herself, buxom and all the brighter for being rained on, was threatening to fly off her board. Light from the pub windows blazed in puddles. The verge was festive with foxgloves and ragwort breaking out like banners. The door of the public opened on a rich whiff from the bar.

Charlie said, 'What's it to be?'

'Whatever you're having.'

He would have liked Scotch, but two, possibly four, would set him back. 'I'm having bitter.'

Senga said, 'I love beer.'

The barmaid remembered Charlie and asked if he was suited.

'Yes, thanks. I got into the hotel you told me about. The Bellechasse.'

The barmaid raised her eyebrows, already over-hooped. 'Well, you would.'

Taking her first pull of beer Senga asked, 'Why don't you get paid for your pictures?'

'I've yet to find out what people will pay for.'

'Do they want the sort of thing I saw in your car?'

'I don't know what you saw.'

'Listen,' she was excited, 'someone who painted man-eating babies and people with pigs' heads has just died. He was Greek or Polish, you must have heard of him. I can't remember his name – it began with Z – Zorbo or Zanzi or something.'

'Zeuxian?'

'Yes, well, collectors are queuing up to buy his work—'

'He died around 400 BC.'

'I said I can't remember his name!' Charlie saw the function of the yellow flecks in her pupils. They lit up when she was roused. 'I'm trying to help. If it's just a question of style—'

'You think I'd be better as a faker than an originator?' Charlie was suddenly angry with generalities and the tolerance accorded artists like himself – would-be creators and bringers of reason. In a small way – there was no big way – he sought to invoke reason in his brush-strokes.

'I didn't say that! Don't put words in my mouth. The best thing you ever did – what was it?'

'A nude. Of my wife.'

'Ah.' She waited, digesting it. 'What happened to her?'

'She divorced me and married a house.'

She blinked at him, believingly. 'So what will you do?'

'Try to get a loan from her.' Not the ideal solution. 'She owes me, at least her husband does.'

'Her husband – the house?'

'He goes with it.'

'Where do they live?'

'The other side of Truro. I'll go as soon as my car's fixed.'

'I could take you.'

'Thanks, but no. If I were to drive up with a girl beside me Nina not only wouldn't believe I'm skint, she'd see me damned before she'd part with a penny.'

'Don't worry, I'll keep out of sight.'

When he had first glimpsed the valley of the Fal Charlie felt he ought to do something about it. The combination of hanging woods, dark water and white mud had started the old sequence: first the spark, then the flicker and the long slow burn. He had begun working out how to catch the bilious colours in the shallows.

'China clay,' said Senga, 'washed down from the workings. That white stuff reminds me of clowns.'

'A grin on the face of the waters – if I could get that!'

'Would you like to go down to the creek and take a closer look?'

'I don't want to look close but I shan't feel I'm in the picture until I've got the gist on canvas.'

She pulled into a lay-by and lit a cigarette. 'What's the name of where we're going?'

'Tregurgle, or gargle, Tre-something.'

'The nude of your wife, was that your only way of getting into her picture?'

Charlie said softly, 'Can we push on? Through the village and over the bridge.'

'I've never made contact with a graphic artist, a re-creator. Writers, yes, I've had experience of journalists, that ilk. Their images are ephemeral but a picture's conclusive, you can look at or leave it, you can't argue with it.'

'You can. I'd like to get somewhere with El Greco, but his people look as if they've only been half-digested.'

'I'd like to get somewhere with you, Charlie.' She laughed: Leda and the Bird pressed against his thigh.

Surprised, he said lightly, 'I'm accessible,' but he shifted in his seat.

She drove out of the lay-by, they shot through the village and on to the bridge at speed. The bridge was old, with barely room for one horse and cart to cross at a time. Charlie held the edge of his seat to steady himself.

They drove in silence, for which he was grateful. He needed to prepare his encounter with Nina. He wasn't even certain of the way to Mellilot. He kept thinking he recognised something but the lanes were lookalikes. Passing a dead hedgehog he was sure it was one he had seen before; its front paws were lifted beseechingly but in vain, and he had been sorry about that. Then they emerged on an A-road.

'Which way?' Senga demanded.

'Left.' He felt a pull in that direction. Half an hour later another hedgehog scuttled across the road under their wheels. Senga swerved. 'I hit it!'

Charlie got out to look, saw the avenue, the yews and beeches, the gate, the name. 'You missed it. But this is the house. This is Nina's.'

She peered at the gate. 'Mellilot?'

'If you don't mind waiting here I'll walk up.'

'I'll wait, but if you're too long I'll leave you to walk back to the hotel.'

She parked in front of the gate and was lighting another

of her cigarettes as he started along the drive. He was visited by the thought that if Nina had not returned from lobbying in London he would have to lobby J.T.

He saw her – for the first time in five years – on her haunches with her back to him, delving in the basin of a non-playing fountain. Nina, wife of his bosom. His bosom reacted with a couple of sharp raps on his sternum. It seemed she, too, was informed: he was still yards away when she looked round.

'Charlie!' She sounded pleased as well as surprised. Rising and coming to meet him, she said 'Charlie!' again, positively joyful. He went to take her outstretched hands, not caring they were muddy, but she snatched them away to wipe on the seat of her bright pink jeans.

'You always hated pink,' he said.

'Time for a change.'

She herself was changing. He noticed a scarlet craquelure on her cheeks which had been so creamy-white. Her hair, which had been inky-black, was highlighted with yellow streaks.

'This is lovely.' She put her arm through his. 'Thank heaven you had the decency to come back.'

'Come back?'

'The times I've wished! Then you came when I wasn't here.'

'I came to see J.T.'

'He told me. He told me why.'

'I've had a feeling, you could call it a scruple, ever since we broke up.'

'Come and have a drink.'

Remembering how alcohol mellowed her, he let himself be steered towards the house. He was aware of affluence as soon

91

as he set foot inside. There was a smell, impossible to define; simple home-loving couldn't provide it, it cost money. It came from Afghan rugs, cigars, good wine, beeswax. And Nina's perfume. Once, while they were married, in a moment of passion and desperation, he had bought her a phial of Arpège and she was still addicted. That hadn't changed.

He sat on an over-stuffed, over-floralised settee overlooking the terrace. 'Why were you grubbing in the fountain?'

'It's a lily-pool and needs cleaning out. You'd be surprised what ends up in a lily-pool besides lilies.'

She gave him a large whisky. He said gratefully, 'How was the lobby?'

'Successful. We brought the minister to his knees. He's a small man, about two inches high. There were women who kept baying and yelping as if it was a fox-hunt. Rather distressing.'

'You were always soft-hearted.'

At the end, she had disciplined her heart against him; he had better be prepared to find that had not changed, either.

'Tell me what you've been doing.'

'Scraping canvases together for a show when I can afford a gallery. I hope you'll come.'

'Why did you let J.T. have my portrait in the nuddy?'

'I couldn't think who else it should belong to. I meant to give it to him, but he insisted on paying.'

'Too much, he said, but wouldn't tell me what.'

'Thirty guineas.'

'Why did you accept?'

'I was taken by surprise.'

'It was an insult.'

'I didn't think the price was quite right,' Charlie said mildly. She splashed more whisky into their glasses: indignation made her reckless. 'I left London with the intention of making a meaningful gesture. The more I thought about it, the more meaningful it was – a far, far better thing than I'd ever done.'

'What do you mean?'

Charlie, who hadn't gone into it in depth, now tried to do so. 'That picture is a testament to you.'

'As a sex symbol.'

'As a woman, as everything a woman should be. And you were.' He pressed her knee, earnest, not lubricious. 'It was wasted, turned to the wall in my studio. It doesn't belong to me any more, it belongs to your husband. I wanted him to have it.'

'So you can compare notes.'

'What do you think I am?'

'A fool. He would have paid anything to keep anyone else from seeing it.'

'We both feel like that.'

Nina ran her fingers up and down her glass, looking thoughtful.

Charlie took a swig of whisky. 'I came here reckoning on turning round and going straight back. But my car's broken down and I've had to put up at a hotel.'

'You could stay here, at Mellilot.'

'I don't think J.T. would approve. The fact is, I need ready cash to pay for repairs. I can't use my card, the bank won't give me any more credit.'

'Hard times?' She was crisp, dismissive. Listening might

be as far as she was prepared to go, plus tea and sympathy – or just the whisky. 'Which hotel are you staying at?'

'The Bellechasse, a little family-run place. Until I can get the car repaired.'

'How did you get here?'

'I had a lift.' He voiced the thought which had been uppermost in his mind. 'He said he was going to burn it.'

'He hasn't.'

She was with him, always had been when it came to his work. He felt a glow in his bones which outshone other considerations, including the money. Even the money. 'I miss you. You were the only one who knew what I was trying to do.'

'I often wanted to do it myself.'

'I bet he doesn't give you moments like that.'

'Charlie, my darling, if you're jealous, my cup will overflow.' So saying, she emptied her glass. 'Another for the road? You're not hitching, surely?'

Suddenly the glow was gone, leaving him as he had been, less than he had been. Miserable. Whisky did that to him.

'Stay for lunch.'

'I can't. There's someone waiting.'

'Waiting?'

'To take me back, a fellow guest from the hotel.'

'He can stay too.'

'We have to get back. Thanks all the same.'

'Come when you've got your car fixed and talk to J.T. I'll get you the right price for my portrait. It's worth at least five hundred to a connoisseur of nudes.'

'Would you care if it went to someone like that?'

'Why should I? You painted what you saw and no one else has seen.'

'Suppose J.T. burns it?'

'He won't until he's done looking at it. Come back tomorrow.'

'Someone said the big end's gone. Isn't that the worst that can happen to a car? I may have to dump it.' His eyes watered. 'Why do we drink this stuff?'

'John Barleycorn the golden.' Nina herself was riding high.

'God knows when I'll see you again.'

'Have the garage send me the repair bill. You can pay back when you're able.'

In a gush of emotion he sprang up to take her hands and drew her to him. But over her shoulder he sighted Senga crossing the terrace.

'Come tomorrow,' said Nina, 'or the next day or the next. But come.'

'Did you mean what you said? About the garage bill?'

'I want to see you!'

She folded against him. He lifted her arms from his neck. 'Someone's coming.'

'Damn!' She went to the window. 'Who on earth's that?'

'A girl from the hotel.' Nina had a way of shutting her face. He hadn't seen her do it for a long time: it was an eminently unhelpful sign. Under his breath he cursed Fate which was screwing things up. 'She was kind enough to drive me here.'

Senga came in, held out her hand. 'Mrs Mellilot, I presume?'

The evening meal had been enlivened by the Claphams

waiting at table. They kept the swing door into the kitchen permanently swinging, passing each other with laden trays and uncooperative cries. Eashing and Mildred felt unable to give undivided attention to their food.

Afterwards Felicia Soulsby delivered a lecturette on what she called the uncoefficiency of the Bellechasse.

'The kitchen is outdated. All working surfaces should be of synthetic material, unproliferating plastic.'

'I find no fault with the catering,' said Mildred.

'I give you Mrs Clapham's a good plain cook, traditional to a degree. Certainly not nouvelle cuisine.'

'I have never been attracted to foreign dishes.'

'I'm no foodie,' said Felicia. 'The point is, our good Mrs Clapham could do with more help.'

'Now that the greater-busted Bet has flown,' remarked Senga.

'Flown?' Progressively and systematically deprived of his faculties, Eashing had every reason to be sorry for himself and little sorrow left over for anyone else. But now he was vividly reminded of Bettony, her diligent breathing as she came to his table and the miscible kitchen odours she exuded. 'Flown where?'

'Back to Grandaddy. They live in a council flat.'

Mildred said thankfully, 'That's nice.'

'The old man was accustomed to spit in the fire when they lived in a cottage. Now he spits at the central heating, one of his more mentionable habits.'

'He isn't unkind?'

'He only beats her when she breaks something.'

Felicia said alertly, 'So there's a history of breakages?'

'The poor kid's cack-handed.'

'She has psi-faculty, common in teenagers with mental shortfall.'

Eashing said, 'You're saying she's feeble-minded?'

'Mentally disadvantaged. She has had an unpropitious upbringing, it takes understanding and patience to supplement low IQ.'

Eashing turned to Senga. 'How do you know about this grandfather?'

'She told me. She's not so dumb. People see her as a kitchamajig and don't bother to talk to her.'

Eashing, too, was used to being overlooked, his immobility taken for insensibility.

'I have been content to observe,' said Felicia. 'Interrogation and interpretation must come later. A premature approach can do permanent harm to the psyche.'

'Interrogation? Interpretation?' Eashing struck at his useless knees. 'What are you getting into?'

'Psychobabble,' said Senga cheerfully.

'The paranormal is of profound interest. I have made a study.'

'When is the normal para?' said Antony Wallington.

'That,' said Felicia, leaning on it, 'is the million-dollar question.'

Senga appeared to take a cigarette out of the air. Eashing, who was watching, saw that it came from behind her ear and had been concealed under her hair. 'She just needs to be noticed: you'd be surprised what she's noticed about us.'

'Us?'

'All of us here. This place is the world to her, she doesn't know any other to compare it with.'

'Pam says she's felt someone watching her.'

'I have tried to engage Bettony in conversation,' said Mildred.

'What will she do now she's lost her world,' wondered Eashing.

Felicia Soulsby turned her star-spangled glasses on him. 'You underestimate her potential. The world of the paranormal knows no boundaries, it is rich and strange. I find it *épatant*.'

'Clapham's already advertised the vacancy,' said Wallington. 'There's a notice on the gate – "Help wanted".'

'A telekinetic teenager is not an asset in the kitchen,' concluded Felicia.

Piper picked up the phone. Sam said, 'Yeah?', his greeting to friend and foe alike.

'Where have you been?'

'To the pictures.'

'Who with?'

'My circle, from the church.'

It was news that Sam had a circle, or a church. 'What was the film?'

'No film. We went to the National Gallery to look at pictures of Jesus.'

'Someone here paints pictures of trees rising from the dead. And someone else is showing undue interest in my affairs.'

'I didn't tell her where you are!'

'Don't shout. I can deal.'

'Can I come and see the trees rising from the dead?'

'Not just now, Sammy. I'm too busy. What was she like, the girl who wanted to know where I am?'

'Like?'

'Was she tall, short, fat, thin, dark, fair?'

'How should I know? She came through on the blower.'
Sam was sulking.

As they walked in the rain, the girl had told Piper, 'You and
I are two of a kind.'

'What kind is that?'

'We're both journalists.'

'I see myself in the role of counsellor.'

'"The Listening Ear" – "The Prying Eye"?'

Piper had a prospectus prepared for cavillers. 'I recognise
the need which was previously supplied by family life and has
been sadly lost in this day and age. The need for confidant,
adviser, *friend*. So many people are isolated by circumstance
and the materialism of modern life, they need to share their
troubles. The knowledge that someone, somewhere, *cares*,
can make a postage stamp the price of a life. I have had
letters from people on the brink of suicide.'

'Yes, I've seen them.'

'You read my page?'

'If I have to.'

Tasting salt in the air, Piper had a presentiment. 'How
did you know where I was?'

'I had the salient fact from your editor.'

'He had no right to divulge it.'

'He thought it might be good publicity. I've been com-
missioned to do a series of articles on the usage and abusage
of the cult figure through the ages, back to Merlin. I'd like
to start with you.'

*   *   *

99

When she was not at breakfast next morning, he asked Mildred Gascoigne, 'Where's your friend?'

'You mean Senga?'

'Your niece, perhaps.'

'I have no brother or sister. She's not actually a friend. We've only just met. Friendship takes longer.'

He wondered if she had left the hotel. But of course she wouldn't. She was going to write about him. Mildred wondered why he was interested in Senga, gave herself one guess, and grieved.

Clouds were building over the sea, gassy yellow shapes steadily advancing before a too-warm wind.

'Weather's on the blink, Miss Gee,' Clapham said to Mildred as she prepared to take her newspaper into the garden.

'Oh dear. Perhaps it will improve this afternoon?'

'I wouldn't bank on it, coming in from the sea.' Clapham shook his head.

She summoned her courage – really it was absurd, she scolded herself and rehearsed what she would say before she went up to Piper's room in the tower.

She tapped on his door, but being invited to enter, hesitated in the doorway.

'Miss Gascoigne, please come in,' he said.

'Am I intruding? Do please say – You won't remember – I wrote to you – "Perplexed, Bromley". I have never forgotten your reply, it was so warm and understanding. You quoted a poem: "Love is not love that alteration finds". It was so *right*.'

100

Piper was familiar with the alterations love found. He hadn't dared to stand and fight them, he had lost so many battles, cravenly let himself be driven away.

'Mr Piper, may I seek your help now in a small matter? Quite trifling, really,' she broke off, flustered. 'I was planning a visit to one of the National Trust gardens, but the weather is deteriorating and my entrance fee would be wasted – here one has no recourse – I would have expected some provision for indoor pastimes—'

Piper wondered if she was going to suggest hide-and-seek or hunt the slipper. He said, 'Personally I am relieved to find no electronic games installed.'

'Oh I do so agree! I was thinking of Scrabble, Ludo, non-competitive pursuits such as jigsaws—'

A through-draught blowing round her obliged him to lay restraining hands over the papers on his table.

'Of course you have your work and I am disturbing you. It's really such a trifle—'

He had heard someone describe Mildred Gascoigne as looking like a rabbit with no ears. He now saw how apt the description was. He said, 'Perhaps you will tell me what your problem is.'

'If I might consult – if you have it with you – I mean – your dictionary. I am trying to finish the *Daily Telegraph* crossword and I have racked my brains – I do hate being beaten. It's frivolous of me to interrupt when you are so busy.'

'Not at all. What is the clue?'

'It reads: "Public vehicle reversing would diminish a country

residence but portend a wedding". The only thing which fits
is "cottabus". Is there such a word?'

'Let's see.' He leafed through the dictionary. 'As a matter
of fact, you're right. Cottabus was a game played by young
men in ancient Greece. He who threw the most wine into
a wine-jar was accounted lucky in love.' When he smiled at
her, colour rushed up from her collar-bone. '"Bus" being the
vehicle in reverse becomes "sub", otherwise "inferior" – refers
to "cotta" short for "cottage", the country residence.'

A gust of wind, gathering strength as it was channelled
through the tower, slammed the door to, shoving Mildred
bodily over the threshold and hunting loose sheets off Piper's
table. They flew up like birds, flattened themselves on walls
and ceiling and fell, twitching, into corners. It was as if the
room went wild.

Mildred, on her knees, tried to retrieve typewritten pages
from under the table.

'Please,' Piper said. 'Leave me to restore the sequence.'

'Oh dear, I am so sorry—'

He put out a hand to help her to her feet. 'It has allowed
us to get acquainted.'

Reading in the garden, Eashing was distracted by a sudden
darkening of the page. Someone, a heavy breather, was
stooping over him. He recognised the breaths: they had
often tempered his soup.

'You all right, mister?'

'Thank you, yes.'

'You looked dead.'

'I'm not quite. Yet.'

She bent lower: he felt as well as heard her breath. 'You don't want to talk like that.'

'What are you doing here?'

'I work here.'

'I understood not any longer. Did they give you due notice?'

'She took against me. But Mister C's been good to me.'

Eashing said he was glad to hear it.

'There's a storm coming. Better get you inside.' She swung his chair round, hauled him backwards up the steps, talking all the way. 'He didn't want me to go. "Don't you forget our good times. I never will", he said, "I never had such times, only with you."'

Eashing was struck by the pride in her voice and didn't know which of them to be sorry for, her or Clapham. On the whole he thought she was the most deserving.

As she wheeled him into the lobby a hot wind went before. Leaflets pinned to the walls lifted horizontal, the rotating stand displaying postcards of local views spun round like a top.

Mrs Clapham rose from the reception desk, mottle-necked and glaring. 'You!'

Patently she was addressing Bettony, but Eashing replied. 'It seems a storm is brewing: we've come in for shelter.'

'I told you, miss, to stay away from us!'

'Bettony was kind enough to help me indoors. I might otherwise have been exposed to drenching rain, to say nothing of thunder and lightning.'

'You wouldn't, I'd have come myself to fetch you.' Mrs Clapham was making dismissive gestures as though she were shooing chickens. 'Off you go, girl, no hanging about.'

Eashing could not see Bettony's face, but heard her sniff deeply. The door slammed. He said, 'I'm afraid she'll be caught by the rain.'

Mrs Clapham's neck condensed to a unified wine colour. 'She'd walk dry if the sky fell.'

'Why are you bolting the door?'

'Against the storm.'

When Pam Wallington first dreamed the dream it stayed with her all day: nothing else could get through. She kept coming over sick and faint, her body behaving as if it was trying to expel something. She had believed it was only one night's nightmare, but all that day was aware of imperfection, as if she had the power of seeing to a faulty source.

The dream kept recurring, undimmed. She tried recapturing the worst moments in her mind, hoping to see them in a different light. Because there must be hope, the source which had produced dinosaurs and phased them out in favour of humans surely must get it right in the end.

Then it *happened*. She had walked down to the creek in the very early morning, she had just had the dream again and couldn't bear to stay in bed. She felt cut off, targeted. The rest of the world was asleep and she was on her own. A tree stump blocked her path. It had been a big tree; the slab of wood that was all that was left of its base was several feet across. Antony said you could tell the age of a tree by the rings

in its bark. She didn't want to know how old this tree had
been. She pushed through the shrubbery to where the light
was, over the sea. The air around her was still grainy from
the dark. The grains gathered in hollows. Rhododendron
leaves licked her bare arms. How easily a bush becomes a
bear. She thought, Where did I hear that?

She had reached the point of asking the purpose of
the dream, why it kept coming – once would have been
enough. The obvious answer was that it was a warning.
Someone, or something, was trying to warn her, her own
flesh and blood perhaps, she had been all hints and nudges
since coming to this place. Perhaps the obvious answer was
too obvious. Weren't dreams supposed to work in reverse?
Dream of the dead, hear of the living. Having dreamed of
the partly living, must she face the wholly dead? Or was it
a sort of riddle? Or a trick to alert her to one threat while
setting up another much worse? Was she being threatened
with the loss of Antony? The sickness of her heart became
a stranglehold. She broke through the shrubbery on to the
shingle. The tide was turning, petticoat frills rolled round the
headland. A cabin cruiser, scabby with lichen, bore the name
The Maid of Orleans. Burned at the stake, did she know that
was coming?

Pam looked into the boat. The wheel was secured by a
tarred rope; plastic coverings of the seats had broken loose
and hung in shreds; visible through the gaps in the bottom
boards was a wash of cloudy yellow liquid.

The dream began. Beneath the surface of the liquid, only
just beneath – it was so light, weighed next to nothing – was

the thing she had been obliged to cradle in her arms night after night. It was coloured by the waters in its wooden womb: it looked up, eyeless, stretched its buds of arms in entreaty, turned its faceless head and cried, soundlessly, from a non-existent mouth.

A bird called, 'Philip, Philip, Philip' from the shubbery. Pam ran for her life.

She made the mistake of telling Antony. She hadn't the words for it. They stayed inside her: horror, revulsion, bitter, bitter dismay, fear and anger. 'I'm so frightened!'

'What of, for God's sake?' Antony spoke as if she was talking about spiders.

'It just lay there under the water – it had no legs—'

'A mermaid. Was she pretty?'

'It wasn't finished, it shouldn't have been born!'

'You've got a sick imagination.'

'I didn't imagine! It's there in that boat, *The Maid of Orleans*, down on the beach. Go and see for yourself—'

'I shall. This sort of thing puts me right off you.' He grinned, his eyes hard.

Owen made a start on the garden. He bought a book about weeds so that he would know what he was up against. The glossary fascinated him: he pored over lanceolate, panicle, pinnate, apomictic, eleistogamous. When it came to identifying individual species, he was alarmed. Flourishing in his patch were things with such names as Goutweed, Twitch Grass, Coltsfoot, Fleabane, Black Medick, described as obnoxious and virtually ineradicable. The good old dandelion he welcomed as Taraxacum officinale, and the little lawn daisy as Bellis perennis.

'I was hoping to find a root of agrostemma githago.'

'Why?' said Elissa.

'It's a sort of wild carnation. The seeds are poisonous. In the Middle Ages it was thought to contaminate cereal crops and cause leprosy.'

'Are you trying to frighten me?'

He started to say 'My dear girl' but bit back the words. 'The plant is extinct as a weed and only survives where it's cultivated – which it certainly hasn't been here.'

'You've changed.' She had a way of quizzing him from time to time: he could actually see her weighing his pros and cons and reaching some conclusion which she never imparted. As a young husband, ardent and unsure, he used to beg her to tell him what she was thinking: nowadays he was truly thankful that she wouldn't. He believed they had achieved the right degree of ignorance to sustain a happy marriage. 'Since we came here,' she said, 'you're different.'

'Be odd if I wasn't. You said yourself it would be like turning a page.'

'I haven't changed.'

He escaped to the garden. Stinging nettles, he was reliably informed, had been leaving their seeds and pollen in deposits since before the last ice age. They had adopted the reproductive system which kept the human race going: male and female flowers were on separate plants, but they didn't have to wait for close encounters. Cross-pollination was by air

107

current. Cooked, he understood, they were indistingishable from spinach and a source of Vitamin B. He was reluctant to cut down such an enterprising plant.

'You want a billhook for that lot.' Mrs Latimer had come with her elevenses into the garden.

'I'll manage.' He wondered if he would when the blades of the shears rebounded from the stem of an oak seedling. He tugged at it, poked round the root with the points of the shears. The seedling would not budge. He feared it was already well enough established to be clocking up the first of its seasonal rings.

Mrs Latimer watched him pluck a handful of grass to clean the blades. 'If you don't mind me saying so, you're not cut out for manual labour. Bank manager, weren't you?'

'Not exactly.'

'I didn't think to see you grubbing in the dirt with them filbert nails.'

Confound the woman, thought Owen, and moved away towards the fence. He had mixed feelings about the fence. It was the barrier between himself and Angela, a stern reminder that the fibres of his being had rejoiced. The jubilation was best forgotten. He owed that much to Elissa.

At one o'clock it came on to rain and he was glad; he had been hacking away for hours without making any real impression. When he tried to straighten he was seized in a grip of fire. It was impossible to stand upright. He sank to his knees, crouched groaning under a clump of cow-parsley and was obliged to witness in close-up the evacuation of an ant-hill which he had disturbed. He shouted, but was too far from the house to be heard. Gritting his teeth, he struggled up, a knee at a time. He crept across the garden with a red hot poker at the base of his spine.

Elissa scolded, 'There's no need to overdo it. What are you trying to prove?'

'We're landowners now, I'm accepting responsibility for the land we own.'

'Shouldn't you accept that you're not as young as you used to be?'

'Do you think I haven't?' Wincing, he lowered himself into a chair.

'I've got some excellent liniment. I'll rub your back and bring a hot-water bottle.'

'I'd sooner you brought the whisky bottle.'

'The garden's bad for you.'

'Someone's got to tame it.'

Next morning the pain had subsided, except for a savage jerk on what he supposed were his hamstrings when he stooped.

Elissa had driven into town to do the weekly shopping. When she was out of the house he allowed himself to remember the jubilation. He owed that much to Angela. She had revived his vital urges to match her own: the time-honoured function of young women who took elderly lovers. He had reached that bleak conclusion when she knocked at the door.

'I can't find James. Is he with you?'

She had come through the wet grass in her thin house-shoes. Seeing her on the step, rubbing one foot against the other, Owen's logic evaporated. He drew her over the threshold, heard himself say, 'Elissa's not here.'

'I know, I saw her drive away.'

The relevance of that did not escape him. 'And James isn't here.'

'It happened, didn't it? Our loving?'

'My dear – I'm not likely to forget.' She came close. He said, 'Shouldn't we look for the boy?'

'I have looked. He hides.'

'Hide and seek?'

'He doesn't play games with *me*.'

'We'll try the garden first.'

'He isn't there, I've searched.'

'The tool-shed? Do you think he's in the house?'

Impatient, she took his arm. 'Come.'

Owen said as they walked across the grass, 'I found him sitting in the road, remember?'

She went straight into her bedroom, threw off her coat and her shoes, came to him where he waited in the doorway and stood in her stockinged feet on his feet. He fancied he could hear her heart beating somewhere below his ribs. 'What about James?'

'He won't have gone far.'

Reaching up, she brushed her lips against his, lightly but with increasing ardour. He held her elbows. 'I should have left a note for Elissa, she'll wonder where I've got to.'

'Do you want her to know?'

That was the question – like Hamlet, he thought, and

stooped to kiss her. Pain hit him in the small of his back. Transfixed, he could only stare over her head. 'There's something in your bed—'

'What?'

'I saw the bedclothes move.'

She drew away, turned back the eiderdown. James lay curled underneath. 'What are you doing here?'

'Waiting for you.'

Owen saw his face. His expression was ugly: in a child, frightening.

'Good as new,' said the mechanic, switching on the ignition. The car leaped forward and was braked with a stylish screech of the tyres. A puff of smoke, pure as a rabbit's scut, issued from the exhaust.

'I didn't ask you to make it new, I asked you to make it go.'

'There's a towing fee, and VAT.'

'That car was original,' said Charlie. 'Every part contemporaneous. It never needed a distributor, why should it start now? And what's the coil for? Family planning?'

The mechanic turned to the small print on the back of the bill. 'No responsibility can be accepted for mechanical defects of replacement parts occurring outside the specified running-in period.'

'What's your time worth? Fifty pounds an hour? I'll pay you twenty-five cash to cover the half-hour you spent screwing screws.'

The mechanic, who had a ponytail and a gold ring in his

ear, smiled sourly. 'Payment by cheque and/or Visa must be cleared with the issuing bank.'

'I'll just take it for a trial run.' Charlie held out his hand for the ignition key. The mechanic put it in his pocket.

'No repossession of vehicle until repair bill's settled in full.'

Back at the Bellechasse, Charlie worked off his emotion on his sketch of the tree escaping from the cliff. He blocked in the background with winged furies, thickened the slender twigs to a head of bristling hair and did a mountainous sea rolling in on a beach of skulls.

There was still Nina. He telephoned: 'Remember what you said about my car repair bill?'

'What did I say?'

'That you'd pay for it.'

'I did?'

She sounded surprised. Whatever well-springs of feeling the offer came from had dried up.

'It would only be a loan. I'd pay you back when my show comes off. Ordinarily this wouldn't present a problem, but the garage have had their fingers burned and are touchy about cheques. And I didn't bring a lot of cash.'

Whenever he spoke to her on the telephone he used to ask what she was wearing so that he could picture her breathing. He had seen it so often and never tired of it. At each intake her bosom lifted to a precise degree of perfection before sinking to rest in her ribcage. But J.T. must have bought her a new wardrobe. 'Have you still got the peacock-blue dress?'

'That old thing!'

'It was the beginning of a rainbow.' The dress had picked up skin tones which he had introduced into *Nina Complaisant*. Nina clothed to reveal Nina nude. The colour, strident on its own, was tenderised in her veins and softened to lavender in her crevices.

'Come, but don't bring that girl.'

She rang off and he went to collect the sketch which he had left on a bench in the garden. Wallington was shading his eyes to look at it. 'What the hell's it about?'

'Just creaming off some of my profane thoughts.'

'Don't let Pam see those skulls. She gets funny vibes on the beach.'

'I know, I've had them. I mean to put them over on canvas, a spawn of fingerlings, homunculi, moppets, freaks.'

'She swears she's seen something so bad it's still giving her nightmares. Sort of a giant tadpole so far as I can make out.'

Charlie laughed, but Wallington looked glum. Charlie said, 'My ex-wife used to wake me to tell me her dreams. She dreamed a lot, I hardly ever got a full night's sleep.'

'Pam and me aren't wed. She had a key cut and moved into the flat while I was at the shop. I got back to find her tights drying on the radiator, the fridge full of fat-free yogurt and garlic pearls in the bathroom. It brought me out in a worry rash.'

'Is it the bed thing?'

'I can handle that. I'm actually very fond of her, but she'd like us to be together all the time.'

'That'll pass,' Charlie said knowledgeably.

'She wants to get inside me and throw the switches.'

Pinned to the hotel notice-board was a typewritten sheet: 'There will be a boat-trip to explore the creeks on Thursday, available to guests of the hotel at the special price of £2.50 per head, payable in advance, bookings at reception, cast-off 2.30 p.m. Signed: E Clapham.'

'Shall you go?' said Antony.

'I don't know, I've business on dry land.'

'Come, but don't bring that girl', Nina had said. Mellilot was not on a bus-route, the ferry was miles away, even as the crow flew. Charlie had toyed with the idea of flitting overnight, hitching to Mellilot, and unburdening to Nina. He believed there were in his burden things which could be relied on to interest her, and possibly charm a loan out of her.

Felicia Soulsby said, 'We took a vacation to Louisiana and saw the bayous in the Mississippi delta. Those are some ponds! But I give you your houses. You have the prettiest houses. Blenheim, Warwick Castle, Longleat, Luton Hoo, Hampton Court – I lost my heart to the Chinese dairy at Woburn.'

'You've seen Mellilot?'

'Melliwhat?'

'The jewel of the West Country. Not so big as Woburn, but history in every stone. It dates from early Roman to Victorian England.' Charlie reckoned he could say that with some truth: the Rape of the Sabines was – or had been –

featured on the terrace and there was the wagonette in the stable yard.

'Guess I've had enough history. I need to freshen up.'

Charlie said thoughtfully, 'It's not generally known that Mellilot was the direct inspiration of the best-selling novel *Rebecca*.'

'I tend to read biographies. That film was popular entertainment, a contrived representation of the morbid psychoses actuating a man who couldn't manage his wife when she was alive and was crazy for her when she was dead.'

'Mellilot *was* Manderley.'

'It was burned down.'

'In the film. The present owners don't talk about the things that are still going on. They have a lot to put up with.'

'Such as?'

'Ghostly voices, cold draughts, weeping women—'

'Malarkey. Incorporeal beings cannot speak, or weep or leave the yard door open. Such phenomena as are experienced by the living have been attributed to the dead out of ignorance and the refusal to look into our own depths – whence cometh sin.'

Charlie feared he had been wasting his time. What did he hope to achieve with such a yarn?

Felicia, a tall woman, drew herself to her full height and her glasses glittered. 'Where is this Melliwhat?'

While he was eating lunch Charlie considered what he should do with her when they got there. He could leave her in the car while he went ostensibly to enquire if they could visit the house. With luck – not to be relied on – he would have presented Nina with the repair bill and thought of a watertight excuse to get back to the car before Mrs S's patience ran out. He could then explain that the house was shut up, the family away and no visit possible. The difficulty was the watertight excuse – finding one. If he told the truth, Nina would be sure to go to the gate to check who was waiting for him, and seeing Felicia Soulsby, by no means an unpresentable woman, would assume he had unrestricted access to every female at the hotel.

The drive proved eventful, the events being a road-holding contest with a Massey-Ferguson earth-mover, a girl on a restive horse, a road gang with a tarboiler and a herd of cows which Felicia failed to take into account until the last split second because she was intent on delivering a child's guide to psychotic phenomena.

'Fear of the unknown is in point of fact fear of oneself. When one's sensibilities peak, there ensues an upsurge of extra-sensory perception. It is as simple and as beautiful as that. How much happier we should be if we accepted it!' How beautiful would it be, mused Charlie, if they ended up flattened like the hedgehogs? 'We are all born with inner percipience, though few of us have the power to use it. My husband's sensibilities are hopelessly blunted.'

'Shame.'

'In the business world he need look only as far as the next buck.' She spoke with bitterness.

Charlie said, 'Everyone has to take the short view sometimes.'

When they drew up outside the gate she saw the padlock and said, 'How very unwelcoming.'

'Naturally Mellilot's not open to the public, it would be bound to attract sensation-seekers and the media. I'll walk up to the house. I happen to know the family and when I've explained your interest is legit they'll be happy to show you round.'

'I'll walk with you.'

'Let me talk to them first. They're sensitive about the things that happen here. I'm sure you can understand that.'

'I shall want to know what happens.'

Charlie climbed over the gate and sprinted up the drive.

Nina was wearing the peacock-blue dress. A sign that she was prepared to be co-operative? The first thing she said was, 'How did you get here?'

'Does it matter? I'm here and it's just the two of us,' Charlie said warmly. 'Like the old days.'

'I don't want to talk about the old days.'

'They weren't so bad, were they? We had good times.'

'You don't have to soften me up. I know you're here for the bad old reason. Money.'

'I don't recollect ever asking you for money.'

'You didn't need to ask, you just never had any. It was as simple as that.'

She sounded like Felicia Soulsby. Nice, Charlie thought, to be able to dispose so easily of two seminal questions, sin and money. 'This is a purely local situation. I have great expectations in Golders Green, but here they don't believe in them.'

'Cornish folk like to see the colour of your money.'

'If I can't get home I can't raise the money and if I can't raise the money I can't get home.' He tried to keep it light: when she saw the bill, it was going to get weighty. 'You're looking well, married life suits you.'

'It didn't suit you.'

'Why do you say that?'

'You've shed ten years since we parted.'

'I get more sleep.' She looked at him with an old gleam in her eye. He said, 'Where's J.T.?'

'Around.'

'What's he done with your portrait?'

'Hidden it.'

'Nina complaisant?'

'It's not a side of me he's familiar with.'

She was serious. Charlie checked his grin, said, 'If he'd paid me a decent price for it I wouldn't be coming to you now,' which was a mistake. Too late he bit his tongue. The old gleam became a flickering flame. She was going to make an emotional issue of it – the woman discounted. 'I meant to give the picture to you both. I came with that intention because this is where it belongs – you married the house. He made me a derisory price and I'd like to go away and forget it.'

She came and put her arms round his neck and her lips to his ear: the old gleam used to progress from there. But now there was a change, a tensile strength in her arms. She nipped the lobe of his ear and blew into it. Deafened, he tried to detach himself. She tightened her grip, drew down his head and sought his mouth. There was to be another price which he would gladly have paid under different circumstances. He said, 'I never forgot you.' She locked her fingers and made a rope of her arms: Nina commanding. He said, 'Hadn't we better go upstairs?'

They might have gone, and been caught *in flagrante delicto*, and the outcome unnecessarily complicated had Charlie not caught sight of a glitter approaching along the drive. It vanished behind the yews: it could only be Felicia's fun-glasses. 'Someone's coming—'

From the shadows J.T.'s bald pate emerged, steaming into the sunlight. Nina smoothed her hair, drew her dress up over her shoulder – Charlie didn't remember pulling it down. He said urgently, 'What about the bill?'

'What bill?'

'The garage repair bill on the car. You said get them to send it to you.'

She came close, cupped his chin in her hand. 'Little boys mustn't always get their own way.'

It was one of her well-remembered and most disliked ploys. Sometimes she turned it on them both, mimicking a little girl, piped and wheedled and pouted until he was forced to abandon whatever he had been trying seriously to discuss.

J.T., putting his head round the door, found them entwined. 'There's a woman waiting for you, Olssen.'

Nina hit Charlie on the nose.

Piper, making for a quiet corner in the garden, was unpleasantly surprised when Senga fell into step beside him. She

119

was smoking, the habit he regularly castigated in his column. She said, 'Why does every other place-name here begin with TRE?'

'TREOW is old English for tree.'

'Tregony, Trelissick, Tregallow, Trewoon – they have to advertise?'

'It's an indication that this area was once extensively forested.' He stopped before taking the path through the shrubbery. 'Excuse me, I have work to do.'

'I like Brocéliande better.'

It gave him another, alarming, surprise to hear her speak a name which he had thought his own discovery.

She expelled twin plumes of smoke. 'The sacred wood where dragons feared to tread. Where the Holy Grail was buried and Merlin, the first cult figure, was locked up in an oak tree by his lover.'

'I am not addicted to fantasy fiction.'

'It had a bad reputation. Saints, sorcerers, lunatics and pilgrims went into the trees and never came out. Wolves and wild boars made short work of them. People said the way through the wood was the way from earth to heaven. You can interpret that any way you like.'

Piper had been impelled by a hypothesis encountered in a magazine article: 'If one accepts that the land-mass was not always fragmented as it is now, the primordial forests could have extended from Brittany to Bodmin Moor.' The concept of the enchanted woods seemed to promise new perception in his counselling. He said, 'In point of fact there's a place called Greatwood only a few miles away.'

'And fifty million years ago London was all trees. Lest we forget, we've got St John's Wood, Kenwood, Chorley Wood, Hinchley Wood, Wood Green, Wormwood Scrubs . . .'

Piper planned to extol the calmative influence of trees, was already facing the problem of how to invoke their therapeutic properties in high-rise flats and supermarkets.

He said bleakly, 'The theory is ecologically sound.'

'Oh sure. Did you know there are still bits of the old forest at Paimpont in Brittany, just off the N24? They've got a training camp there: the French exercise their tanks and armoured cars in what's left of it.'

He had begun his piece: 'There can be no sight more pleasing and healing to the troubled spirit than the natural rhythm of great trees bending to the breeze . . .'

She said, 'You know I'll have to raise that business of the little girls.'

'I beg your pardon?'

'You were tutoring backward children at the time.' His heart missed several valuable beats, then hammered on his ribs. 'Amanda, Rosealeen and Sue. Three little girls. Remember?'

'I don't know what you're talking about.'

'It rated front pages of the tabloids. Blew over, though, didn't it?'

'It was total slander. I would never harm a child, by word or deed. I received a public apology from the newspapers concerned.'

'My remit is to explore the myth of the Agony Uncle. Whether I explode it or not is up to me. Of course kids are such liars and little girls are the worst. I might leave you with the benefit of the doubt if it made for an intriguing ending.'

He said between his teeth, 'How dare you! Any such inference would be libellous!'

She grinned, unabashed. 'I dare because my editor special- ises in investigative journalism, pulling the wool off people's eyes. His idea is a searchlight on cult figures, anyone who has caught the popular fancy, or a significant section of it – yours is highly significant. You're down to the bottom layer – the born losers who look to you to sort them out. So we'll begin the series with you and work through the media, the glitterati, the royals, and end with one or two of the more charismatic serial killers.'

'I am not a cult figure!'

'In character assessments you can't neglect the libido. It's the first thing you look at. Your name's not really Piper, is it?'

'Piper is a *nom de plume*. Anonymity is essential for the role of confidant.'

'The reclusive, solitary type, fascinating to women – they long to draw you out.'

'I was not aware—'

'Oh come on! Our eligible spinster, Miss Gascoigne, is already in your toils.'

Piper's heart sank. Or was it his stomach turning? He had been nervous about this girl from the beginning – he was deeply alarmed now. Her skin, covered with pale gold confetti marks, effectively modified any change of expression.

With such an advantage she was not to be underestimated. He said stiffly, 'I have a wife and child.'

She laughed. 'You won't get away with that. Your boy, Sam, loves to talk. Lonely people do.'

It was one of the days Mildred thought of as having holes in them, holes in time. Looking into the window of the antiques shop known as Grandma's Tidy the holes were visible between warming pans and stuffed birds and the case of ammonites. It meant that she was made aware of lapsing. There were a few things she had done – walking to the village, looking round the church, buying postcards and a cake of unperfumed soap. She planned to take coffee at eleven, leaving time for a visit to the castle before lunch. It had become necessary to justify how she spent her time, something she did not have to do while at home. As yet it was barely ten-thirty. Half an hour to fill if she kept to her plan of walking up to the castle after coffee.

The last time she had stood looking through the window-sockets at the view she had experienced a compulsion to think herself back into the past and had succeeded to a certain extent, though the past was comparatively recent and the history her own. She had recalled, with painful clarity, the moment at her father's funeral when he had made his final gesture of rejection.

He sent a gust of wind which plucked her wreath from its privileged place on his coffin and bowled it across the churchyard. One of the undertaker's men went in pursuit. It was a pretty wreath of red carnations and yellow roses, bearing her message: 'In loving memory . . .' She had tried loving, it was her duty and he was the only one she owed it to, she had tried, had *wanted*.

The wreath came to a halt beside the standpipe where people filled their vases. As the undertaker reached for it, it rolled gently into a puddle. By the time he brought it to the grave, muddied and battered, her father's coffin had been lowered out of sight.

She had come to, her chin on the crumbling stone of the castle wall, and tears in her eyes. A darkening over the sea which had been mirror-bright did not reassure her as to the time factor. How long had she remained propped in that undignified position?

Grandma's Tidy promised a happy medium: no need to ponder on the ammonites, their past was unthinkable. She went in, determined not to be prevailed on to buy anything she did not want.

At first glance it seemed there was nothing she, or anyone of normal disposition would want: moose's heads, African voodoo dolls, glass walking sticks, a garishly painted ship's figurehead built to – literally – breast the waves. Mildred averted her eyes, and so doing caught sight of something which caused her heart to leap and sink simultaneously: a collection of medals displayed on dark blue velvet in a glass case.

She went close. They reminded her how little she needed reminding, how close to the surface of her thoughts he still was. In years nobody had come closer yet stayed so distant. She was brought face to face with the fact, and

124

what it entailed. The hole in the day filled with the knowledge.

'Can I help you?' The shopkeeper was at her side. 'Are you interested in gongs?'

'Gongs?'

'Allow me.' He depressed a catch on the lid of the display case. 'These range from the Crimea to the Falklands. A truly representative collection. Here's a genuine Iron Cross Second Class with the original ribbon and swastika – the swastika must be removed if the medal is worn now. Here's an Air Crew Europe Star: the silver rose means service as the crew of fighter planes during the Battle of Britain. The Victoria Cross is an excellent replica. You can read the words "For Valour" under the lion and the crown.'

'I have some medals at home. They were my father's.'

He looked at her, adjusting to the fact that she was not a likely customer. 'You want to sell?'

'I would never part with them.'

The shopkeeper snapped the case shut, an impatient sound.

Mildred said, 'May I look around?'

'Be my guest.' He went and leaned against the counter, watching. She pretended interest, picking up things for a closer look, careful to let him see her put them down again. Moving towards the door, preparing her escape, she took up a small, heavy brass object. 'What's this?'

'A fly.'

'Yes, I see. It's well made, such detail.'

'Should be. They have plenty to copy where that comes

125

from.' He bared his teeth which were younger than he was. 'Genuine Benares paperweight. Four quid. Three-fifty to you.'

'Thank you.' She put it down. 'I'll think about it.'

He watched her cross the road. She could feel him watching; he had nothing much else to do.

'Aren't you the lady from the Bellechasse?' said the waitress in the café, bringing coffee in a pretty china cup and pot to match. 'How do you find it?'

'Very satisfactory, such nice people.'

'Any little upsets?'

'How do you mean?'

The waitress smiled. 'You may be lucky – with the weather.'

At half-past eleven Mildred left the café to walk up to the castle. Sun and sea breeze restored her spirits. Sense, she told herself, was more important than sensibility. The man designated her father was dead, leaving her his kitbag containing his dirty socks, a packet of strong mints probably intended to relieve stomach pains which she had not known he suffered from, and some metal discs engraved with commendations for meritorious deeds which he had never spoken of. No word of love, no tender gesture to remember him by.

Sense was a series of negative responses. Perhaps the answer to everything was nothing. At that point sensibility took over and she was afraid of nothingness, the extent of it, of its engulfing herself.

The castle, knocked about a bit, was still *some*thing, after five hundred years. From the ramparts she watched a man ploughing, pursued by gulls. The way they rose up, whirled and sank, reminded her of Piper's paper-storm and how she had cried 'I am so sorry!' and he had consoled her, 'It has allowed us to get acquainted.'

She hurried down the green flank of Castle Hill. She would say, 'It's to make amend for my clumsiness, a paper-weight to ensure that your work will not be disturbed again.' Three pounds fifty was not too much to pay for the thought: to let him know that she had had the thought.

'I have been so remorseful about the interruption to your work.'

Struck by an implied longevity of her regret, Piper said dryly, 'I trust it hasn't spoiled your holiday.'

'Oh no, indeed not. It was such a trifle – not the interruption, I mean; that must have been extremely aggravating. I keep remembering.'

'There is no need.' When she gazed at him in silence the likeness to an earless rabbit was quite pronounced. 'I have forgotten the incident.'

'I have not. Your papers all disarranged, displaced by the wind – because of me. Inexcusable.'

'Don't give it another thought.'

'Will you accept this small atonement?' She proffered a package wrapped in tissue-paper.

'I assure you it isn't necessary.'

'Please take it.'

He did so, reluctantly, unwrapped the package and held

on the palm of his hand a brass fly with wings outstretched.
'Why are you giving me this?'

'It's a paperweight, to prevent your work being disrupted
in the same way again.'

'How very kind.'

'It has happened before: on that occasion it was a message
from my father.'

'Indeed?' Piper turned the thing over in his hand, disliking
it on sight.

'He was communicating his feelings from the grave.'

It was not unreasonable for Piper to experience a downrush
of tedium. He was so often called on to counsel the bereaved
that the sense of loss, he had concluded, be it of fame, fortune, or loved one, was a paramount human emotion. It was
certainly the most frequent. He prepared to hear yet another
tale of dispossession. 'You had a cherished relationship with
your father?'

'I had no relationship with him. He had no time for me.
He wanted a son.'

'Fathers and daughters are privileged. They see their children grow into womanhood with delicacy, compassion and
tenderness – the qualities of the gentler sex.'

'If only that were true!'

'You don't believe women have those qualities?'

'My father did not see them in me.' She spoke with har-
boured bitterness. Piper thought that to be born a daughter
to a man desirous of a son was unfortunate, and doubly so for
one lacking feminine charm. 'He was a professional soldier.
After my mother died he lived in barracks and sent me to

lodge with a Mr and Mrs Boddington and their family of
three boys. I hardly ever saw him.'

'As an army man his free time would be limited.'

'He used to play football and cricket with the Boddington
boys. I could never think of anything to say to interest him.
I was still a child: I did the only thing I could think of – I
tried to be a tomboy.'

Piper said, 'Do you want to tell me about it?' and suppressed a sigh.

She turned away to hide some too potent memory. 'I
wasn't cut out for it, I'd always liked being clean and tidy.
Trying to keep up with the Boddington boys was a failure.'

And shaming, the start of a long lease of shame. She could
never forget how she had run about when there was nowhere
to run to; how, when she banged doors as the boys did, Mrs
Boddington, a caring woman, asked had something upset
her; when she got her shoes muddy the mud disgusted her;
when she shouted they all stared; when she climbed a tree
she came over giddy.

Piper was listening – the Listening Ear – and surely he
was seeing it too, her utter humiliation when she had tried
to join her father and the boys at football. Because she had
no proper clothes, she had put on her wellies and tucked
her hair under a beret and run on to the field. Her father
stood stock-still when he saw her, his jaw dropping. The
boys, who were kind, shouted to her to go into goal. They
sent a slow ball. She threw herself on it as she had seen
them do, and fell flat on her face. The ball trickled past the
goal-posts, the boys cheered. She scrambled up, bleeding

from her nose. Her father walked off the field. The memory still sickened her.

'I didn't see my father at all between the ages of ten and twenty. He was posted abroad. Once he sent a picture postcard of camels kneeling. On the back he had written "Funny beggars"'. No signature.

'I left school and went to secretarial college. He paid for everything, there was never trouble about money. I got a job, moved into a room of my own. He sent a small regular allowance.'

'You wrote to him?'

'He didn't answer my letters. Once he rang up, said we'd better meet for lunch, as if it was something we often did. I hadn't even known he was in the country. "We're off to North Africa," he said, "there's a little account to settle."

'I worried about what to wear for our meeting. He hadn't seen me for ten years. I decided on a tailored suit and blouse with a bow tie. I cut my hair short: no make-up, I went with a shiny face.'

Ten years had brought him to early middle age, some fierce white flecks in his hair and a thickening of his neck. The rest of him was still hard and wiry. A seam of something, tension or vigilance, had opened between his eyes. She wanted to touch it, felt she could have eased it out.

'He looked at me, I thought he's really looking, for the first time. He said didn't I have anything nice to wear. "A dress. Your mother wore a dress and she always looked nice."'

'It was an indication of his concern for your future.' Piper introduced a kindly twinkle into his eyes. 'No man is entirely indifferent to true femininity.'

'The next time I saw him he was in a military hospital with a tent of blankets over his body. I was upset, I cried, "What is it? What's happened to you?" He said, "The fortunes of war." I said, "There is no war." "There's always a war," he said.

'He didn't die of wounds: he contracted an obscure Eastern disease which dried him up, a sort of drought of the body fluids. At the funeral his comrades came to me and said he had been a good friend and a fine soldier. All he left was his medals. I don't even know if he meant me to have them.'

'Have you never thought perhaps they were all he had to leave? Courage is manifest in its immediate context, in the eye of the beholder; those medal discs are his only evidence to you and the rest of the world of the sacrifices he made and the dangers and hardships he endured. They constituted his life's savings.'

'I wanted something personal to remember him by!'

Piper adjusted his tone to one of gentle rebuke. 'The strong man is silent; when he can't express his deepest emotions he takes refuge in his masculinity.'

'I never asked him for anything.'

'He could not give, you could not ask. There were constraints on both sides. Do you condemn him because for all his bravery he feared to speak three small words: "I love you"?'

Face to face with Mildred Gascoigne and accustomed as he was to conducting his sessions on a paper-to-paper basis:

'Write to The Listening Ear, enclosing an s.a.e. . . .' – he wondered if he had gone too far.

Her eyes filled, she sniffed – or was it a sob? The telephone rang.

'Excuse me.' He turned to it thankfully.

Sam said, 'When are you coming back?'

'Soon.'

'I never knew why you went to that place.'

'I can't talk now.'

'Someone with you? Is it that girl who was asking about you?'

'There's nobody here.'

Piper hung up. He looked round.

Mildred Gascoigne had gone. He sat for a long while idly turning the brass fly in his fingers, disliking it still. Now that he came to think, wasn't his situation the same as hers? Neither of them had been capable of inspiring love where love was due. They had both made fools of themselves in the attempt. An act of charity would have saved her, but where had he, the counsellor of love, gone wrong? Discovering that he had not yet put away childish things was to have been the bond between himself and James. But it had become a barrier, with James – and Angela – on the other side.

On the day of the boat trip a fingering wind blew offshore. The creek built up into a series of travelling ribs and travelled out to sea: there was a business air, yet nothing doing.

'Choppy,' said Charlie.

Clapham, stepping out of his boat, wiped his boots with

handfuls of grass. 'This here's bilge, collected while she's been beached. I'll have to pump her out.'

Charlie assumed that scales of lichen and green veining on the hull were evidence of different waters and conditions. He was impressed when Clapham boasted that he had converted the engine from a Ford car.

'What did you do about the gearbox?'

'Put a reversing propeller in its place.'

Charlie said thoughtfully, 'Is there a market for car engines?'

'Depends what you call a market. I got mine from a breaker.'

'You had to pay?'

'Fifty nicker. Why?'

'Just curious to know what mine would fetch.'

'Are you talking about the vehicle that's been in Penweathers' yard all week?'

'Battery failure. That engine would drive the Queen Mary.'

'I don't advise you to try flogging it. There are plenty of good motors going for a song in the holiday season. Short of the ready, are you?'

Clapham sounded sympathetic but Charlie was taking no chances. 'Idle curiosity. Like I might ask why you call your boat *The Maid of Orleans*.'

'The previous owner's choice.' Clapham polished a brass rail on his sleeve. 'I've a fair bit to do to her. Don't want the ladies getting their frocks dirty, do we?'

In the event, it was Antony Wallington who got dirty. There was trouble between him and Pam. She pleaded with

133

him not to go on the tour of the creeks, but suddenly he was determined that they both should go. They argued about it through every mealtime, even breakfast. At breakfast Pam took to whimpering and weeping; Antony was alternately red-necked and white-jawed. They did not exhaust the subject; it seemed that nothing else could engage their attention and when they were silent the air between them raged.

Soulsby said to Felicia, 'It's a boat-ride they're debating, not the National Debt.'

They went down to the jetty hand in hand, lover-like. Mildred, watching from her window, was glad they had resolved their difference. But when the time came for Antony to help Pam into the boat it was obvious that his hold was a grip of iron, not love. He pulled her across the jetty crying, 'Come and look, sweetheart!' He leaned into the boat and turned, holding up a sheet of plastic. 'See this, folks? Under water it looks like a big tadpole, no legs, no arms, no face, like an embryo before it's legal. Isn't that right, Pam?'

'Leave it be!' roared Clapham. 'It's to keep the ladies' shoes clean.'

Cuddling the plastic, Antony stepped over the side, slipped and slid feet first into the bottom of the boat. Clapham, who was urging Pam on board, effed into her ear; Charlie went to Antony's assistance; Senga and the Soulsbys watched from the jetty.

Flat on his back, Antony groaned. 'What did I tread on?'

'Guano,' said Soulsby.

Clapham fumed. 'I spent all morning scrubbing off the

muck and those bloody skuas did a slash-round as soon as my back was turned.'

Senga said, 'They eat other birds.'

Pam approached, looked into the boat and shuddered.

Charlie held out a helping hand to Antony. 'Oops-a-daisy.'

'I can't – I can't move!'

Pam got into the boat beside him and tried to lift his head.

'Leave me alone!'

'Let him find his feet, he'll get himself up,' said Soulsby.

'I can't! I've broken my back!'

'Oh God!' Pam covered her face.

'I'll take your shoulders,' said Clapham.

'I tell you I can't move!' His voice rose to a scream. 'I'm paralysed!'

Clapham shifted a coil of rope. 'You sat down arsy-versy. No bones broken. The deck's clear.'

Antony closed his eyes, murmured 'Paralysed', lingering on each syllable.

'He can't be – can he?' moaned Pam, still hiding her face.

'Tickle the soles of his feet,' suggested Senga, 'and you'll find out.'

'Try sitting up,' said Charlie.

Antony whimpered. Felicia Soulsby said to her husband, 'See if you can help.'

'Me?'

'It's the least you can do!'

'If he's caused real damage it's best not to move him.'

'You know what I mean.'

'I don't like it.'

'Maybe I should start the engine,' said Clapham. 'To encourage him.'

Antony screamed, 'For God's sake – you want to kill me?'

Pam burst into tears. Mrs Soulsby poked her husband between his shoulder-blades. 'George!'

Soulsby stepped into the boat. His manner was that of a man reminded of a scruple he would prefer to forget. Antony opened his eyes: Soulsby stooped and looked into them. He seemed uncertain what to do next, or whether he should do anything at all.

Charlie said, 'We should call an ambulance,' and Pam moaned.

Antony cried, 'Don't touch me!'

Soulsby unfastened the collar of Antony's shirt. Antony stopped turning his head from side to side and lay still.

'George!'

Soulsby slipped a hand under Antony's neck. Everyone waited. A bird with a malevolent eye flew down and perched on the gunwale. When Clapham lunged at it, it flew away, throwing them a honk of derision. Antony reached for Soulsby's hand and pulled himself to his feet. He stood looking round in a baffled sort of way. 'Lot of fuss about nothing.'

Pam cried, 'You scared us to death!'

'I pull a muscle and she talks about death!'

Senga said, 'Can't we up anchor or cast off or something?'

Mrs Soulsby demanded of her husband, '*Now* do you believe me?'

'No.'

'When proof has been vouchsafed? What more do you want?'

'I don't want.'

'That makes it right? How utterly selfish! You spare no thought to suffering humanity – you could give life—'

'How often have we been through this? Do I have to tell you again, it's a fluke. Fluky!'

'After what's happened?'

'Nothing happened.'

'I just don't understand. You're a thinking man, and caring, but you won't acknowledge this power. Don't you realise it isn't yours to withhold or bestow, you're merely the instrument—'

'Bollix.' Soulsby went and sat in the stern.

The offshore wind dropped, leaving a flat sea with navy-blue cloud shadows. Holding to the bank, Clapham made for the headland. They passed a series of narrow valleys brimming with pink and purple rhododendrons: hidden water-courses emerged from the chaparral to form pools fringed with yellow irises. There was a gradually increasing concourse of pines on the slopes, and inland on level terrain a solid wedge of oak and beech with a dark underpinning of yews.

'Pretty, eh?' said Clapham. 'I told Miss Gee she'd be

missing a treat. She said she couldn't trust herself on the sea.'

As they drew level with the headland the temper of the water changed. Instead of a succession of travelling ribs it piled into combers, white-topped, slapping the hull.

'We're running into a storm,' said Felicia.

'Something big's come into the bay and we're meeting the swell. If there's a blow coming we'll soon know. The Devil's Tooth they call the Point. Many a boat it's chewed up.' Clapham spun the wheel jollily. 'Hundreds of wounded from the Peninsular Wars were drowned hereabouts.'

Soulsby said, 'I read somewhere that gun-decks in the British Navy were painted red to lessen the shock of seeing so much bloodshed.'

'George, you should be resting. It's always the same after one of your sessions.' Felicia turned to address the company. 'My husband has a gift. He denies it, but you can all bear witness that it exists.'

'Just forget it,' said Soulsby.

The boat rolled gracefully, presenting first to port, then to starboard, and finishing with its prow in the air like a playful dolphin.

'She loves a romp,' said Clapham.

They watched him spinning the wheel with what they hoped was competence. Charlie and Senga were thrown together. Antony rushed to the side and leaned over.

'I don't mind this.' Senga settled into Charlie's arms.

He took the opportunity of looking closely at her pigmentation. 'I think I'd like to paint you.'

'Why?'

'To find out about you.'

'There are other ways.'

'It would be my way.'

'What did you find out about your wife?'

'If a painting's any good when it's finished I'll have learned something about myself as well as the sitter.'

She said soberly, 'Promise you'll tell me what you've learned.'

Charlie shook his head. 'If it doesn't work out I won't have learned anything and neither of us will want to look at it.'

Uttering a maritime shout, Clapham steered into open water. The wind smacked the boat on its beam, precipitating it towards the shoreline which bristled with rocks. 'Gunwallow ahoy!'

Felicia Soulsby was pitched forward to a suppliant position on her knees.

'I've been sick,' announced Antony Wallington.

Clapham left the wheel to look over the side. 'Sardines are rising to the bait.'

The boat made for the rocks. Felicia screamed, 'Water's coming in!' and they all saw the gunge on the bottom boards rapidly thinning to a soupy wash.

Clapham said, 'She's carvel-built, it takes her a day or two to tighten up.'

'The boat's leaking, we don't have two hours, let alone two days—' Soulsby dropped his hand on the wheel beside Clapham's. 'Turn around.'

'We'll all be drowned!'

'There's no cause for alarm, ladies—'

'We paid to see the creeks,' said Charlie.

'Get us back to the jetty!'

Clapham looked round at them for confirmation. 'Is that what you want?'

'If you don't,' said Soulsby, 'this tub's going to take us down to the oceanbed.'

Clapham said 'The wife put you up a picnic tea to have on the headland watching the yacht races.'

'No headland, no picnic,' said Soulsby.

'She won't be best pleased if you take it back untouched.'

'I guess not,' said Mrs Soulsby.

'Have it here, on the jetty. You can still see the yachts.'

'There's nowhere to sit.'

'There's grass.'

'I'd rather not,' said Pam Wallington.

Clapham said, 'There's a nice flat tree stump, the ladies can sit on that.'

'I don't care where I sit,' said Senga. 'If there's tea, let's have it.'

'Not here.' Pam turned away. 'Tony – this is where I saw it – in the boat—'

'It's where you made a fool of yourself.'

'I think we should open Mrs Clapham's lovely picnic,' said Felicia. 'We don't want her to think we didn't bother.'

'There's two thermoses,' said Clapham, 'cucumber and paté sandwiches and a batch of tarts made this morning.'

'Is that Mr Eashing over by the shrubbery? He might like to join us.'

'He's asleep, having a sweet dream.' Senga unstrapped the picnic basket. 'Gather round everyone.'

'Are you planning to paint the view?' Wallington said to Charlie.

'It's too well connected. Boats showing their bottoms, woolly white clouds and blue water. Needs to be disrupted. By a figure. Or a tree.'

Clapham said, 'I had to take the tree down. It blocked the view. First thing people ask is can they see the sea from the windows. Pity. Bit of history that tree was. A jerry pilot came down in it and got strung up by his parachute.'

'What happened to him?'

'Died, like a fly on flypaper,' Clapham said cheerfully. 'Best thing he could have done. He'd have been lynched if he'd been found.'

Pam Wallington jumped up and ran. Mrs Soulsby, who was proffering a cup of tea, received most of it down her skirt. Antony Wallington ran after his wife.

Felicia dabbed at her dress. Soulsby took out his handkerchief but she waved him aside. 'Go and help the old man.'

'What old man?'

Tight-lipped, she pointed to where Eashing, slumped in his chair, had spread his hands open on his knees as though begging. 'He needs help right now.'

'He's sleeping like a baby.' Soulsby would like to be doing the same.

'Did you ever see a baby adopt that posture?'

'Want me to go and sit him up?'

'What I want, what I have always wanted from you, George, is for you to share my concern.'

Eashing was leaning sideways, head and shoulders, lacking support, hung over the arms of his chair. His weight, displaced, threatened to tip the chair: its onside wheels were dug deep into crumbling earth.

'Help him George – you must!' Soulsby stirred. Felicia cried, 'Hurry!'

Soulsby took a reluctant step, but quickened his pace when Eashing's chair canted visibly and Eashing started to slide out of it. Soulsby was in time to take him by the shoulders and haul him and the chair upright. Eashing awoke to find the big man pinning him down. Panicking, he struck at Soulsby's hands.

'Hold still.' Soulsby leaned on him. Eashing cried out, beat his fists on Soulsby's chest. Felicia ran to them.

'Relax! You're safe – my husband has saved you. You were having a bad dream.'

'I was having a beautiful dream. I dreamed I was running through a cornfield, through the ripening corn.' Eashing cried, 'I was *running!*'

Felicia said sensibly, 'That would be bad for the corn. The farmer would not be pleased.'

'I can't run!'

'Have you tried?'

'I assure you, madam, for as many times as I have tried, I have failed.'

'Try now.'

'Why?'

'My husband has touched you and he has healing in his hands.'

'Felicia!'

She stopped over Eashing, her sparkling spectacles closing in on him. He lifted a finger to them. 'Don't they deflect your vision?'

'What?'

'I am wondering if these pretty rhinestones distort as well as decorate. I hope not.'

Felicia frowned. 'I don't find my spectacles distorting. But I urge you not to dismiss my husband's gift without giving it a trial.'

A moderate man, with no wish to be more, Soulsby often asked himself how come he had married a woman who had a rapport with supernature. She didn't know when to stop. It was the one thing calculated to worry him. He had strong qualms about what she was trying to do.

Felicia told Eashing, 'You weren't there when Mr Wallington fell getting into that dreadful boat and injured his back. George healed it with a touch. Your dream – why not try to realise it?' She held out her hands. 'Rise up and walk!'

'I won't be responsible,' said Soulsby.

'In Tunbridge Wells we witnessed a miraculous event.'

'I wish you wouldn't keep bringing that up!'

'It's there, George, it's always there. The unknown quantity.'

'Nothing was proved. It antagonised people, they didn't understand and they weren't happy—'

'*I* am happy, I am relieved, I am reassured, I am eternally grateful for my lack of understanding. Have you thought what it would be like if we understood? If we knew what goes on?'

'That business in Tunbridge Wells damn near caused a riot.'

'That business, as you call it, was a miracle which you performed. And that,' Felicia said bitterly, 'about wraps up my uniformity. I mean, why should you, of all people, have the gift?'

'There is no gift!' Incensed, Soulsby snatched off his glasses. 'The kid in Tunbridge Wells was acting blind. When I passed my hand before his face he blinked.'

'Naturally. All at once he could see. You can't imagine what that was like, coming in out of the dark, seeing for the first time his mother, his home, the world!'

'He kicked the dog!'

'He was scared, he didn't know how a dog was going to look, he didn't know how anything was going to look.'

'Why do you do this?' cried Soulsby. 'Aren't I enough for you?'

'The first time it happened was on our honeymoon. Don't you remember? I twisted my ankle, you took it in your hands and I felt healing flow through me.'

'That wasn't healing, that was sex.'

'George,' on a floodtide of memories, Felicia took his hand, 'you were always enough for me. But you have this

144

power and you owe it to the sick, people in pain, children, the aged – it's given to so few, you don't have to be a saint to have it, you must use it to lessen the world's suffering—'

'Christ!'

'Like Him, yes.'

Eashing remembered his dream. He was a boy, arrow-swift, ephemeral and golden as the corn. His feet did not bend the corn-stalks, he was running on air, he had no past to covet and no future to fear. He gripped the arms of his chair, pulled himself to his feet and saw the ground rise to meet him.

'The Bill's here, Miss Gee,' said Clapham, appearing at Mildred's elbow as she was returning from her walk.

'I beg your pardon?'

'To talk to you. Detective Superintendent Plod of the local fuzz.'

'You mean the police?'

'Been parking on a yellow line, have you?'

'I don't drive – oh dear – what can he possibly want?'

'Like me to ask?'

Her hand flew to her throat. 'No—'

'He's waiting in the entry.'

The policeman was sitting with his hat between his knees, reading the hotel brochure. She feared he wasn't going to stand up when she went in, but after a moment's appraisal of her, he did, causing the basket chair to explode with a series of pistol shots.

His uniform – any uniform – mortified her. It stood for indignity and rejection. She said bravely, 'What can I do for you, Inspector?'

'Constable. You won't mind answering a few questions?'

'If I can.'

'You've been to the village?'

'Several times.'

'To the shop called Grandma's Tidy?'

'Yes.'

'When was the last occasion?'

'Yesterday morning.'

'Why did you leave your name on the counter?'

'Because the shopkeeper wasn't there. I went to fetch an item which he had priced for me. I left the money for it, with an explanatory note. I couldn't wait, you see, because my bus was about to leave from the Square and they only run every hour—'

He held up her note. 'Is this what you wrote?'

'Oh dear – did I do wrong?'

'You saw nothing unusual?'

'Only that the shop was unattended—'

'You were not aware that the shopkeeper was dead?'

'Dead? Oh no – he couldn't have been!'

'While you were writing your note he was lying behind the counter.' Horrified, she could only stare. 'The till was old-fashioned, like everything else in the place. It had been forced open.' He took out his notebook. 'But you did not notice.' She uttered a croak. Having trouble with his ballpoint he did not look up. 'What about the hunting-knife?'

'Knife?' The enormity of what he was saying – inferring – began to dawn. 'I saw no knife. I saw no one!'

'The item you took, what was it?'

'A brass fly – oh you don't – you *can't* think—'

'You were seen leaving the shop in a hurry.'

'I had nothing to do with this – this awful thing!'

'Awful! Why do you say that?'

'The man – that poor man – robbed and murdered!'

'Murdered?'

'The knife – you said there was a knife!'

'Used to prise open the cash drawer.' When he leaned towards her she felt it was the readying of a predator about to spring on his prey. She cried wildly, 'You can't think that I – I had to run for my bus – there would have been blood—'

'Have I mentioned blood? Can you produce the item you took?'

'I haven't got it – I gave it as a present.'

'Who did you give it to?' He rephrased the question with a hint of jocularity, 'To whom did you give it?' and she saw the claws of the predator unsheathed.

'A friend – someone staying here—'

'A brass fly? Funny thing to give anyone.'

'It was a paperweight.'

'Ah.' He nodded, with conviction. 'Can you produce the friend? To corroborate your story.'

Mildred found that she was wringing her hands. 'I would rather not involve him—'

'His name, if you please.'

* * *

Piper, called away from his column, his communion disrupted, found himself being interrogated by a policeman about Mildred Gascoigne and the wretched paperweight. Would he confirm that she had given it to him? And for what reason?

'Does there have to be a reason?'

'An anniversary? A birthday, perhaps? In recognition of a favour?'

Piper said sharply, 'It was a kind thought. May I know what this is about?'

'Certainly sir. A local shopkeeper has been found dead on his premises, the till broken open and rifled. Miss Gascoigne, by her own telling, was one of the last – could have been the very last – person to see him alive. I am trying to establish the facts and clarify the situation.'

'Oh Mr Piper!' cried Mildred, 'I am sorry, it's all my fault. The shopkeeper wasn't there when I went back to buy the paperweight – at least I couldn't see him – and I was in a hurry to catch the bus. I left the money and a note saying I'd taken it – the paperweight, I mean – I knew what it cost because he had already told me – I didn't know he was under the counter – dead . . .'

Mildred dissolved, literally Piper thought, into tears. They coursed down her cheeks: surprising how much liquid small ducts could secrete. He said, 'Is this a murder enquiry?'

'That,' said the officer, writing in his notebook, 'is a matter of opinion. A technicality. The deceased was known to have a chronic heart condition. Threatened by an assailant with

148

a knife he might have died of fright. One thing is clear: somebody knew he was dead and took advantage of the fact to break into the till.'

'Why would I do that?' cried Mildred. 'Why would I leave my name and address and money for the paperweight if I was going to rob the till?'

The policeman scratched his nose with his biro and suggested, 'To divert suspicion?'

Detecting a ribald undertone, Piper said sternly, 'As a professional psychologist, and student of human nature, I assure you this lady is incapable of such duplicity—' and encountered Mildred's drowning look of gratitude. 'I suggest you give serious thought to some more likely suspects.'

'Well, we're not short of mischief around here.' The policeman's biro ran dry. Vexed, he snapped it in two.

'What's up?' said Clapham, coming into the lobby as the policeman crunched away down the drive.

Whey-faced, Mildred stammered, 'I – it's nothing—'

'A computer error,' said Piper.

'When do you want me to sit?'

'Sit?' Charlie, in the garden, was sketching Eashing, slumped in his chair.

'For my portrait. I shan't be here forever.' Senga leaned over Charlie's shoulder. 'That's not bad.'

'I shan't need sittings, the way I'm going to do yours.' He was feeling none of the usual eagerness to get started on it: was conscious of something like technophobia. 'Head and shoulders –' head certainly, get through her carapace, resolve the maculae – 'it has to be different, not just what Joe Soap sees. I want to take an inward look. There's no such thing as whole truth; doing Nina's portrait showed me that. The most I can hope is to reveal what no one else has seen.'

'And if I don't want it revealed?'

'I'd like to do it as a strip cartoon. Be different, wouldn't it?' Her skin darkened: he was intrigued to see the freckles merge to produce an overall colour, just short of puce. 'No offence: the cartoons I'm thinking of aren't comic pictures, they're preparatory drawings, working designs. I see your portrait as design.'

'I'll look like wallpaper. Why don't you paint Piper?'

'Why should I?'

'To illustrate the biop I'm writing. I'll need a good likeness. Look, why not come back with me, to London? We could stop on the road, make a night of it.' Her stare, luminous as a cat's, held him and he thought, I should paint her from a mouse's eye view.

A car swept through the gate, spitting gravel. A woman got out, legs followed by a leisurely unwinding until she was revealed, one hand on the car roof, the other on her hip, sales-effective, like girls in car adverts.

'Nina!'

She was wearing champagne colour, a dress of some clinging stuff which the breeze pinned on her like a second skin. Charlie told Senga, 'This is private,' and tried to move away from her.

'She can stay.' That was Nina imperious. 'Obviously she has your interests at heart.'

'I have to talk to you.'

'I have a puncture, it's why I'm here, so you can fix it, Charlie.'

'You know I've never changed a wheel.'

'Darling, it's simple. I'd do it myself but I'm not dressed for the part. I'm on my way to give a talk to the Pennyworthal Conservationists.'

'What about?' said Senga.

'Disappearances.'

'Which ones?'

'Threatened species.' She turned to Charlie. 'Suddenly the steering went puddingy, which suggested a puncture.'

'If you're worried I could drive you to Pennyworthal,' offered Senga.

'*I'll* drive her,' said Charlie.

'Not in my car, darling.' Senga tweaked his ear fondly. 'Besides, I'd like to hear that talk. Hold on while I fetch my keys.'

They watched her go, Leda and the Swan rioting as she went. Nina said, 'She hasn't the legs for shorts.'

'Let's take your car and go before she comes back.'

Nina looked at her watch. 'It's too late now.'

'I don't believe you were going to Pennyworthal or wherever. You came to check on me.'

She closed her eyes as if she had reached the end of an interminable tether. 'I'm a conclusively married woman. The days of wine and roses are over.'

Thinking he heard a note of nostalgia he hastened to turn it to advantage. 'There's nothing between her and me – how could you think there was?'

'I'm not remotely concerned with your amourettes.' She slid into the car.

'Nina, wait!'

Sending a kiss off the palm of her hand, she drove away.

Eashing wrote to his solicitor: 'I have found a girl. She was, you might say, under my nose – like the object of most searches – having been employed in this hotel until she was dismissed for breaking crockery. She is not well washed, but she is strong, and by nature vegetal, she will do nicely for the short while I shall remain here. Fellow guests are supportive, but I do not enjoy being wheeled about like a helpless infant, I prefer to retain a degree of control over my exits and entrances.'

'I could shave you,' Bettony had said. 'I shave my grandad. He's warty but I've never bled him. I'll do you if you want.'

'Thank you, no. I'm letting my beard grow.'

'It makes you look old.'

'I am old.'

'Not as old as my grandad.' It sounded like a shortcoming. She sat down beside him with a sigh which threatened to empty her body of breath.

'What's the matter?'

'Nothing.'

'Would you like to read the paper? There's an article on

the woman's page about the moral refreshment to be derived from sweeping a room.' Eashing smiled grimly.

She accepted the newspaper and he went back to his book. When he looked up again she was rolling the paper into a tube. She held it to her eye. 'Nelson!' Eashing couldn't remember ever before seeing her laugh. The eye watching him from outside the tube glistened with fun, her mouth opened to reveal big crooked teeth.

'Perhaps you'd prefer the magazine section.' He retrieved his newspaper and was unrolling it. 'Or a work of fiction?'

She shook her head.

'Don't you like to read?'

'Can't.'

'You can't read?'

'Nor can't my grandad.' Manifestly, the pride in her voice derived from the old man, occasioned by him. He was her exemplar.

Eashing said carefully, 'I'm sure he manages well enough without. But times have changed, it's different for you. Without some basic literacy you will find yourself severely inhibited in the workaday world.'

She declared from under a beetling brow, 'I can work!'

'Of course. But books not only add to the quality of life, they define it,' a point he would have liked to make, but could see she wasn't taking it. He could hardly expect her to.

'She is uneducated and taciturn,' he wrote. 'They are recommendations. I shall not be exposed to the tedious chatter of semi-literates.'

He forbore to mention the fact which had come to light

153

by chance: she scorned literacy, but loved being read to. How much she realised of *Oliver Twist* – Eashing's holiday choice – he had no way of knowing, but she hung on the words and when Eashing closed the book and asked, 'Did you like that?' she had uttered again the prodigious sigh which seemed to squeeze the breath out of her. This time it was an exhalation of pleasure. Eashing, too, had enjoyed the reading; it was a shared experience (something he had little of nowadays), besides being edification of a mentality sadly in need.

His decision was not reached so much as imposed. Even if it made only limited sense, it would relieve him of the irksome business of interviewing females whose qualifications did not warrant their travelling expenses.

An escape clause was essential, and Bettony would, he thought (not unkindly) be willing to go back to her grandfather any time he wished to be rid of her – reimbursed, of course, in excess of whatever the Claphams had paid her.

When he asked would she consider acting as his 'companion help' – a quaint way of putting it, he couldn't think of anything else as precise – she blinked, passed her tongue round her lips. The effort to comprehend was proving painful. 'It need not involve you greatly, just to help me in and out of my chair, wheel me to the beach or along the lane, fetch anything I need from the shops, be generally handy.' Eashing smiled. 'Read *Oliver Twist* with me.'

That registered, she nodded vigorously, biting back the chuckle of a child invited to mischief, and dodged under the arm of Mrs Clapham who was bringing Eashing's tea.

It was all the answer he was likely to get, and when Mrs Clapham demanded, 'What's *she* doing here?' he said, 'I have just engaged her as my companion help.'

In the ensuing confrontation, Mrs Clapham declared Bettony to be the Devil's drab, catspaw, jinx, witch and trouble-maker extraordinary. She vowed she had known not a moment's rest while the girl was on the premises.

Eashing said mildly, 'She has a simple mind, incompatible with life in this day and age. But there's no harm in her.'

'Simple she may be, pure she is not.'

'This is an ad hoc arrangement which should not incommode you. We shall take walks and make such excursions as can be organised, and she will be available to do errands for me in the village.'

'I swore I'd never have her under my roof again!'

'I trust,' Eashing said, still pleasant, 'that as a guest – a paying guest – I may be permitted to provide the little extra assistance I need for myself?'

Elissa had asked Mrs Latimer's son to take over the heavy work in the garden. Privately Owen was glad to be rid of the chore but deplored their dependence on Mrs Latimer. 'I don't like the woman, she's a mischief-maker.'

'She's a conscientious cleaner, rare these days, and her stories do enliven our coffee breaks.'

'You've developed a taste for gossip. I call that pretty radical.'

'Why?'

'You said you haven't changed since coming here.'

'You're trying to change the subject. To get back to the one under discussion, old bones can't sustain prolonged physical toil.'

'My bones are still perfectly sound. I happened to set too fast a pace.'

'I have no intention of standing by while you do yourself permanent damage and end in a wheelchair for our remaining years. Mrs Latimer is a country woman: she tells me that the first cut of such long grass should be by hand, but there's a knack to be acquired in the use of a scythe, it's not recommended for novices. Apparently the local doctor sliced through the calf of his leg while working on his allotment and had to bind it with rhubarb leaves to stop the bleeding.'

'Rhubarb leaves are poisonous.'

'Only when they're boiled.'

At first sight he did not look like a wielder of scythes or any such archaic tool. He arrived on a motorbike with blaring exhausts, a sort of computer screen on the handlebars, and a fire-breathing dragon rampant on his T-shirt. He pushed up his crash helmet and lifted his goggles, revealing the cherry-lipped face of a teenager. 'Latimer, Kevin, IFO – Identified Flying Object.'

Owen said, 'What happened to the mountain bike?'

'Gave it to the old lady.'

'Your mother?'

'I'll be giving her this –' he revved the engine – 'soon as I get me a car.'

'Very filial.'

'You kidding? She can't wait to ride it.'

Owen suspected he would be the loser in their exchanges, and turned to the garden. 'Do you think you can manage this?'

'No problem.'

'What will you use?'

Kevin tipped his helmet over his face. 'Be back tomorrow with a couple of goats.' A kick-start exploded to a shattering roar and he was away.

'I haven't much hope of Mrs Latimer's progeny,' Owen told Elissa, 'he's a whippersnapper.'

'She says he's jokey, it's the only thing she's got against him.'

'I don't like his attitude.'

'If he's as good a worker as his mother we can overlook the rough edges.'

'He's no horny-handed son of the soil.'

Elissa shrugged. 'Drive me into Truro tomorrow?'

'What for?'

'The curtains we brought from Wimbledon aren't right here. I must find something different.'

'He's coming to cut the grass tomorrow.'

'You don't have to be present: better if you're not. Your attitude is prejudicial.'

When they returned from Truro the next afternoon, Owen stopped the car and sat staring. Where there had been a blossoming prairie was a rectangle of shorn grass encompassed by a naked fence: a suburban patch.

'Happy now?' said Elissa.

'I prefer the prairie.'

She slammed the car door and went into the house. Owen thought about the fence. Half obscured, it had been both barrier and ethical factor: stripped and fully revealed it looked uncommonly like a pen for penning animals.

Kevin Latimer was raking up the spent grass. 'Get yourself a little Flymo and you'll be able to keep this lot down.'

'What did you use?'

'Billhook and ergocomics.'

Owen looked round. 'Where's the billhook?'

'Mam took it home to peel the potatoes.'

Owen sighed. 'What do I owe you?'

'Let's see. Five hours at eight quid an hour—'

'What!'

'If you don't believe me, ask her next door. She's been watching me, never took her eyes off. Bit of a pain. I mean, you're not always looking for it, are you? I like a bit of tail, don't misunderstand me, but not when it's on special offer. I prefer to make the running myself – stimulates my gonads.'

He leaned on his rake, gap-toothed and happy; no qualms, no reservations, no offence – it was impossible to take any. This was ignorance, and doomed.

'I was querying the rate, not the time.'

'My mam and your missus agreed it. Besides, it was hard graft. I sweated blood.' He held up a finger wrapped in rag. 'Forty quid suit you? Including VAT and doctor's fee for anti-tetanus jab?'

* * *

'You have a visitor.'

Elissa shepherded James before her. He announced, 'I've come to live with you.'

'Isn't it nice?' said Elissa.

James sat in her chair. Owen laid aside the crossword. 'What is all this?'

'She said if you like them so much, go and live with them.'

'It should be fun,' said Elissa.

'James, what's this about?'

'Why are you wearing those glasses?'

'It's rude to answer one question by asking another.'

'We had a row, a real one.' James spoke with pride. 'About the same old thing.'

'What old thing?'

'His coat.'

Owen said patiently, 'Whose coat?'

'My father's fur coat. He used to put it on and we'd play at bear hunts. He was the bear and I was the dogs. I had to go for his throat and try to kill him before he could hug me to death.'

'I thought you didn't like that sort of thing.'

'*She* didn't like it.' James shrugged. 'She used to run out of the house: she won't let me keep the coat. It's his. I've hidden it.'

'In memory of your happy romps?' Elissa said dryly.

'I said I'd go away if she didn't let me keep it. She said I didn't have any place to go and I said I had you.'

'Whatever she said would be in the heat of the moment. We don't always mean everything we say, it slips out, we're sorry afterwards. She'll be sorry already.'

'I'm not.' James came and stood at Owen's knee. 'I like it with you.'

'We like having you but we can't take you away from your mother. It's against the law, we'd have that policeman here again and he'd lock us up. You wouldn't like that, would you?'

James hid his face on Owen's chest.

'Stay to tea,' said Elissa.

After tea, and slices of Elissa's strawberry cream sponge cake, he flatly refused to go home.

'Your mother will be worried, wondering where you are.'

'She knows where I am.'

'She can't be sure.'

'She won't care.'

'Look here, young man,' Owen said sternly, 'I don't know where you get this idea that your mother doesn't care about you. It's wrong, and it's hurtful. You'll know how hurtful when you have children of your own.'

'I won't never have children.'

'Why not?' said Elissa.

'I won't never have a wife.'

Angela said, 'I knew you'd come.'

She took his hand, held it to her cheek. James watched with a brow of thunder.

'We knew you'd be worried. Elissa gave him tea and cake.'

'In that case he can go straight to bed.'

'No!' James hung on Owen's arm, pulling him and Angela apart.

Owen seized him by the shoulders and held him. 'Will you do as your mother wishes?'

'If you'll read to me?'

'Not tonight.'

'When?'

'Tomorrow.'

'Promise!'

'If you go and get ready for bed.'

James went gracelessly. From the door he turned to command, 'Cross your throat and prepare to die.'

She whispered, 'Can't you stay?'

'Better not.'

'You'll come tomorrow?'

'I promise.'

Mildred had found her stroll along the shore dispiriting. On some days, depending on the direction of the wind, the tide deposited shells, arranging them on the sand for all the world as if they were for sale. She had made a collection of cowries and cockles, fan-shaped scallops, striped whelks and some sweetly pretty turret-shells. She found it quite absorbing to wander along, window-shopping, as it were, for half-buried treasure.

But today the tide had brought in much that she would rather not have seen: human detritus from the holiday beaches, broken sand-shoes, orange peel, beer bottles and things the purpose of which was worse than dubious. Obliged to concentrate on her footprints which were immediately obliterated in the wet sand, she fell prey to a mood of dejection, reflecting how little impression she had made on life generally.

After her father died, taking his disappointment with him, there was no one to ask anything of her. I am as I am, she had told herself. Taking her finicalness as strength and her thin skin as a virtue, she had been reasonably satisfied. Overtures she did not encourage. People, on the whole, she found were motivated by reprehensible aims – mercenary, material, sordid. She conserved her deepest feelings.

Was anyone possessed of a pure, generous nature? She was prepared – eager – to give to Piper the benefit of that doubt, for his was the only listening ear. His gentleness reassured her, his good sense sustained her and his understanding went beyond mere comprehension; it lifted a burden she had carried all her life.

How gallantly he had risen to her defence in that dreadful ordeal with the policeman. Kindly, yes tenderly, he had taken and held her hand in both of his. 'There is nothing to fear. And as to your father, you need have no regrets. You are, if I may say so, a personable young woman. This is your life, accept it, embrace it . . .' He had opened his arms and for one dizzying moment she had thought he was about to embrace her. 'Live it to the full!'

When he looked into her eyes, for another dizzying moment she had thought his meaning plain. Then he had sighed. 'Regret is the thief of love.'

Mildred had echoed his sigh. 'I wish . . .' but did not know what she wished or how to say it.

He released her hand, reshuffled the papers on his table. 'I must return to London for an editorial discussion.'

'You'll come back?'

'Indeed.'

One took that to mean yes, verily. He had spoken so gently, chiding her for an unnecessary question. One might trust his manner, but not the word, for she realised that she had often heard it spoken in vexation, mockery – disbelief.

She turned to find the tide spreading like a shawl across the inlet and was forced to dodge an oncoming wave to reach the cliff path. She would say, 'May I ask a favour? Will you bring back for me a copy of the *Spectator*? I am unable to obtain it in the village and I do miss keeping up with the theatre and book reviews.' That way she would be sure of his affirmation.

The door of his room was ajar. She heard him moving about and her heart beat faster. She tapped lightly, called, 'May I come in?'

Senga had up-ended the wastepaper basket on the floor and was sorting through the contents. Shocked, Mildred said, 'Mr Piper's not here?'

'He's gone.'

'Gone?'

'He must be halfway to London by now.'

'Did he say when he'll be back?'

'He's not coming back.'

'But he must be coming back! He's left his work—' Mildred had seen sheets of typescript on the table.

'Discards. He squeezes the clichés till they squeak.'

'What are you looking for?'

'I'm doing a piece about him for my magazine, an in-depth inquiry into his nature.'

'He is a good man.'

Senga perched on the corner of Piper's table and lit one of her inevitable cigarettes. 'At present I've nothing much to work on – apart from the usual frisson about ambivalent sex.'

Mildred said weakly, 'Sex?'

'He claims to have a wife and child. Did you know?'

'I – no—'

'It's a *sine qua non*. To counsel, he's got to know it all, including the husband, father, family man with his problems kept under his belt. D'you see?'

Mildred was trying to.

When Senga drew on her cigarette her freckles glowed briefly. 'Mind you, he has a love nest in Pinner and that's another part of it.'

'Pinner?' Mildred couldn't bring herself to say 'love nest'.

'With little brown Sambo to minister to his needs.' Senga held up the brass fly. 'He left this.'

'It's a paperweight . . .' Mildred's voice dwindled.

'Benares ware. A gift from his little brown lover.'

Eashing wrote to his solicitor and friend: 'I am going to look over the parish church which by all accounts has some promising features. It is but a short distance from the hotel and the girl can take me. She is useful in the way of a willing horse rather than the companion I hoped for. Her world is alien, she is cut off from so much of mine, or perhaps I should say I am cut off from hers. I have had no contact with young people and this poor child has been misused. She tends to adopt a high hand with me, addresses me as "Mister", which I don't care for, but cannot think of any other designation which would be suitable between us. She is as unsure of me as I of her. It leads to some unexpected exchanges.'

He had been reading to her from *Oliver Twist*. She was much taken with the character of Fagin, declared Oliver 'stuck up' and Fagin 'kind'. 'He wouldn't harm a fly. "My dear," he says, like he loves everyone.'

'It's not necessarily a term of affection. Dickens employs it in this connection to illustrate Fagin's devious nature. He is a manipulator.'

'What's that?'

'He handles people so as to make them do what he wants.'

'People make me do what they want but they don't talk nice like him.'

'Fagin's a scoundrel: you're not supposed to admire him.'

She said fiercely, 'Nobody calls me "my dear". It means somebody loves you.'

She was looking forward to their outing and arrived while Eashing was still finishing his lunch.

'What's she doing here?' Mrs Clapham set damson pie and cream before him.

'Bettony is taking me out.'

'We're going to church,' said Bettony.

Mrs Clapham turned to Eashing. 'You realise she can't go inside? Dogs and dummies aren't allowed in church.'

'Despite certain disadvantages, Bettony is a young woman with a capacity for learning.' Eashing pushed his dessert aside. 'If you're ready, Bettony, we'll go.'

'Wait while I put this on.' She produced a straw hat trimmed with swags of orange blossom. 'It's my wedding hat, it was give me by a girl who got stood up at the altar. "You have it," she said, "no one's going to stand you up."' Bettony rammed the hat on her head. 'I know not to go in church uncovered.'

Mrs Clapham went out, banging the door.

'What are we going to church for?' Bettony said as she heaved his chair down the steps.

'I want to look round. Have you ever been in there?'

'I went to chapel till they stopped me.'

'They?'

'They said I sang too loud.'

It still rankled: she spoke with righteous anger.

'You mustn't mind so much what people say, or don't say. None of us choose our words with due regard for how they sound to others. If we did, there'd be much less talk and we'd all be a lot happier.' Platitudinous, but true, he thought.

'It's all right for you, mister, you're educated. Anyway, you're old.'

He said sharply, 'Getting old is a nasty business. There's

nothing to commend it, certainly not the illusion of learning. I have spent a lifetime familiarising myself with one small sphere and I am constantly disconcerted and mystified by my own ignorance. The acquisition of knowledge is illusory.' He heard his bitterness, corrosive self-pity. 'Don't be deceived by talk of tranquil old age: one is not cured of strong emotions. The most ignoble remain.'

'You ought to write that down. I bet you could write good as Dickens if you wanted.'

Eashing twisted round in his chair to see her expression. It was unenlightened; she meant what she said, had no notion of absurdity.

He had glimpsed the church when he was being driven to the hotel. It had a broach spire, and in the churchyard quite a fine Cornish cross. He had written to his friend: 'The Cornish cross, I am told, was discovered late in the nineteenth century buried upside down as a prop for the west wall of the nave! I believe this trip will be more than a mere exploratory venture.'

He wanted to touch the cross, feel the granite, the grit, under his fingers – it was one of the obscure compulsions which he observed in himself from time to time. So much was denied him now in the way of physical experience, minor episodes had to be savoured to the full. He said, 'Take me to the cross.'

'What for?'

'Never mind what for.'

She bumped his chair over the graves without respect for them or for him, and stopped at the cross. He stretched out his hand, laid his palm on the stone, rolled the detritus of centuries under his fingertips. 'Feel how warm it is, from the heat of the sun, the heat of thousands of suns.' She was silent, uncomprehending. He sighed. 'It is so very old.'

'You don't know where it's been.' She seized his hand, briskly scrubbed it on her skirt, and hauled him away over the burial mounds. She put her shoulder to the heavy door of the church porch. As it swung open he noted the wagon roof and was cheered at the prospect of further discoveries.

She wheeled him to the nave. 'Where d'you want to go?' She spoke well above a church whisper. Eashing looked about, hoping there was no one else present. He would have preferred to be alone, and was having to accept, yet again, that privacy meant independence, and his was irredeemably lost. 'Take me to the chancel steps and leave me.'

'I can't.'

'Why not?'

'I don't like it here.'

'You're not required to like it.' He added, more kindly, 'It's no part of your duties.'

She said something which he did not catch, and pushed him, fast, along the nave. He cried to her to wait.

'What's the matter now?'

'I should like to look at the font.'

'What for?'

Never mind, he had said, never mind what for, because there was no way he could explain his longing to touch the old cross. Now he heard himself say, with total irrelevance to this girl, 'I believe it is late Norman.'

168

'What's it say here?' She tapped with her foot on the floor of the nave.

'It's a memorial tablet: "To a Beloved Wyfe, God grant her sweet repose".'

'We shouldn't be stood on it!'

'We can hardly do otherwise. I imagine such tablets were put here in the church to ensure the dear departed a good place in Heaven.'

Bettony sat down in one of the pews. She took up a prayer book, turned the pages, made great pretence of reading for Eashing's benefit, and gave him one of her gap-toothed grins.

His attention had been caught by the carved bench-ends. The design varied for each pew: intertwined foliage and fruit developed from plain English oaks to arabesques of exotic flowers, vines and wreathing serpents. Eden, he thought, must have been a forest.

Having concluded her pantomime, Bettony left her seat and moved along the nave, flattening herself against the pew ends. Her precocious bosom made that difficult, her tongue shot out and curled over her upper lip: she was zealous in her determination to avoid treading on the memorial tablets.

Eashing rolled his chair after her. She came to a halt by the chancel steps, alongside a canopied table tomb. The recumbent marble figure was of a beak-nosed, tight-lipped woman, heavy-lidded eyes closed, hands clasped in prayer position.

'A good example of sixteenth-century English burial furniture,' said Eashing.

'She's in there? Dead?'

'Less than dust by now.' Eashing peered at the inscription. 'It seems this was the local Lady Bountiful.'

'Call me Aunty, she said. Aunty Viv. She wasn't kin of ours.'

'This lady died more than three hundred years ago.'

'I'd never have come if I'd known she was here. She used to wop me with that.' Bettony pointed to the crucifix between the effigy's fingers. 'She put my eye out, my grandad put it back. He used to be a vet.'

'I assure you,' Eashing said patiently, 'this tomb is not of anyone you could ever have known. It is in the standard repertoire of funerary sculpture of that period: the features are conventional rather than distinctive. You may think there is some likeness—'

'That's her, with the mealy face. My mother doted on her. She led my mother into sin. They stole my grandad's savings and ran away together.'

'How very – inconsiderate.' Eashing was at a loss for words.

'I spit on her!'

Seeing Bettony approach the bier, lips pursed at the ready, he cried hastily, 'Please don't!'

'I can't look on that old lady. Let's go.'

'Not yet.'

'I'm not staying with her!'

'I came to see the church and there's much to see.'

Bettony tipped her hat over her eyes and made off down the aisle.

* * *

The rood screen was composed of portions of another screen showing orthodox Biblical scenes and some older carvings of a more liberal nature. He made out a boar with hounds in pursuit, a bear embracing a man and a woman embracing a tree. There seemed something schematic about it but the message, if there was one, escaped him.

As he could not get up the steps unaided he manhandled his chair back along the nave. In so doing, he passed the Lady Bountiful, Bettony's 'Aunty Viv'. Her eyes, which had appeared closed, now appeared wide open; the marble lids had become the whites, blank and blind. The anomaly, of course, depended on how his brain translated the signal from his optic nerve, but Bettony's influence could not be discounted.

How bad, or good for him would she be? In his affliction he tended to seize on trifles and blow them up out of all proportion. Was it unreasonable to hope that his last years would be as equable as possible?

Whichever way he looked at it the effigy was unremarkable. He had seen so many stone ladies in stomachers and ruffs, with the same patrician nose – a requisite of good looks then as a full head of hair is now. His own giving and receiving days were past, but he envied this lady, her giving complete, lying serene on her stone bed to which no dreams came.

He became aware of a movement in his chest, a murmur. He braced himself and was ready when it became a shriek, endured it stoically. There was no room in him for anything more. When the pain ceased and he was still alive, fear took over, the pure and simple fear of not being. During all his researches into funerary concepts he had never felt it so keenly. It seemed to have been provoked by Bettony's identification of this effigy. Surely it was annihilation of the cruellest sort to attribute depravity to someone long dead and in life greatly loved?

Since Bettony had abandoned him – he groaned – he would have to help himself. He leaned forward, bearing strongly on the wheels of his chair, to set it moving. A decidedly uneven slab on the floor of the nave pitched him sideways. His weight did the rest. He toppled out of his chair, caught at the suppliant hands of the Lady Bountiful and contrived to support himself on his knees. More he could not do. After an unavailing effort to get on his feet he achieved only a closer scrutiny of the lettering on the plinth of the tomb: 'A Lady of Beneficence, Piety and Gentilness of Spirit' he read, before a wave of nausea overcame him and he blacked out.

He regained consciousness with the sun warm on his face. Bettony was stooping over him. Somehow she had managed to get him into his chair and wheel him out of the church.

'You gave me such a fright. I thought you'd died, then I thought mister's praying to that witch – then I felt you breathing and I said, "Thank you, Aunty Viv." 'Tis the only thing I ever had to thank her for.' She stroked the damp hair off his forehead. 'Rest easy, mister my dear, I shan't never leave you again.'

*   *   *

172

Charlie was excited. He knew he hadn't been going far enough. The old leap of the heart, the one that always told him when he had done well, told him now that with this sketch of Eashing he had stumbled on something that would take him far beyond adequacy. It would be a big production. At first the empty canvas yawned, the weave so coarse he thought he could never cover it. Then push became shove, and he worked the whole thing out on his sketch block.

It was quite an achievement to suggest colour relations with a stick of charcoal. He had introduced an ambience of emotional gloom: trees that hung, like a bad thunderstorm. He wouldn't fancy walking under them.

Senga had brought Lumsden's canvas. 'You can have this back.'

He hoped for Lumsden's sake it was none the worse for fending off the rain. 'It's not my work.'

'You know I'm going back to London tomorrow.'

'I'll miss you.' He was sincere, not devastated.

She said, 'You'll never do anything here.'

'As a matter of fact, I'm on to something quite different. There are things lying doggo – accredited mysteries which I've never looked into because I've never worked in that bracket. But Blake must have; Dadd, Palmer, Bacon, Burra must have asked What, Who, Why? and got their answers. And I'll get mine once I've rid myself of the old concepts and techniques.'

'It's time you got away. Come with me.'

'Thanks, but I'm going to stay with Nina.'

His expectations had been boosted by a telephone call: 'J.T.'s away at a golf tournament. Come and stay.' It was as good as a promise, practically a guarantee. British Telecom could not damp the kindling in Nina's voice nor stop him catching fire. He had allowed himself to speculate, went through a blissful programme, reviewing and ratifying past memories.

'I'm hoping she'll lend me enough to get my car out of hock.'

Senga's face tightened sequentially, down from her hairline. She said, 'You're not breaking new ground.'

Owen went for a walk, his habit when there was a problem to solve. He needed time for this one. It had come about so quickly, unforeseen and unprovoked. He had always been happy with Elissa and she, he believed, reasonably so with him: they could qualify as prototypes for a successful marriage. Any reservations and disquiets he had felt in his youth had long ago been subsumed by his moderation. He had not expected a great deal and what he now had was enough. He could so easily lose it.

Elissa was fastidious rather than prudish. She disliked untidiness in morals as in anything else, might discipline herself to live with it but would not hold it against him. Her remark about never having been part of an eternal triangle was a veiled warning.

From the end of their lane he glimpsed the pile of old stones – remnant of some sort of castle – beyond the village. He had passed and repassed it in the car and now was minded to take a closer look. Half a mind was all he was prepared to give it; ruins had no fascination for him.

Children were playing in the last of the daylight on the green hill and he wondered if Angela brought James here. He knew so little about their life, how they passed their days, what her hopes for the future were, and the child – what was he waiting for? The old times to return? A stand-in for the man who had fostered his baser instincts and turned his natural affection to enmity?

Boys were chasing a ball under the castle walls: it came bowling down the hill towards him. He stopped it and sent it back with a stylish kick. The boys cheered. He felt uncommonly pleased, exhilarated in fact. Football was good healthy fun, he saw himself introducing James to the game. Angela could not object to such a non-lethal sport and it would bring the child out of his obsession with the past.

He now believed at least part of his problem solved. The other part still weighed on him. He had not coped with his own discreditable feelings. They must be dealt with, suppressed – kiboshed – he told himself.

He had been greatly encouraged by Angela's reaction to his love-making, reaffirmation of a faculty on the wane. Elissa had become tolerant of his failures, dismissive even, sighing, 'Does it matter?' and leaving him unwilling to ask her the same question because the answer was obvious to them both. Confirmation of his own continuing ability in that sphere was gratifying. On the other hand, and under the circumstances, how long would he be able to keep it up? No prudent adulterer living in a village would take as mistress the woman next door, especially if she had a difficult child, an adversary, at her apron-strings.

'Where are you going?'

'To read James a bedtime story.'

'Supper's nearly ready.'

'I promised him.'

'Is this going to be a regular commitment?'

'Of course not. I was coerced. The poor kid was distressed, wanted me to stay last night and read him to sleep. In order to get away I had to promise to go back this evening. He'll be waiting for me.'

Elissa pursed her lips and went on laying the table. 'I'll put your supper in the oven. Don't blame me if it's dried up when you get it.'

Angela opened the door to him with, 'It's been so long.'

'Two days?' Owen adopted a teasing tone. He looked round for James. 'Are we alone?'

'He's in bed. I packed him off early.'

'I said I'd read to him.'

'I've waited, thought of us every minute. I've dreamed – it's easy to be happy in dreams.'

'My dear—'

'You'll stay – afterwards?'

'I'm afraid I can't. Elissa will have supper on the table.'

She made a sound in her throat. An acknowledgement? A dry laugh? 'Mealtimes are quite a ritual with Elissa, she sets the clock by them. In a court of law she'd swear to the time because it was when we sit down to supper.' It was marginally true. Elissa liked the meals she prepared to be eaten at their best.

'Hadn't you better go right away? I'd hate to upset your timetable.'

She managed to sound blithe, but the light in her eyes had gone and he wished he hadn't seen it go: it had been special to himself.

'I promised James. One shouldn't break a promise to a child.'

James said, 'What's she want you to stay for?'

'You've been eavesdropping.'

'What *for*?'

'Just to talk.'

'About me?'

'I daresay we'll find something more interesting.' Owen ruffled his hair, but James ducked and pulled the blanket up to his chin. His face was stony.

'Talk to *me*.'

'Don't you want to hear about Batman?'

'He's a silly bugger.'

'Who taught you that word?'

'I made it up.'

Owen thought the child couldn't be aware of the sexual affiliation: he must have heard and liked the guttural sound and claimed it as his own.

'Look, old chap, don't mind my saying so, but that word isn't altogether your invention. It's been around a long time

177

and it's not a nice word. In fact, it's offensive and anyone you apply it to is entitled to be offensive in return.'

James made a rosebud of his mouth and put up his face. 'Hoo!'

Owen treated it as a question. 'Whoever you apply it to. Now, I'll read you a story about a girl who trod on a loaf and had to marry a frog.'

'Hoo!' James was delighted and disgusted.

'He turned out to be a prince,' Owen said firmly.

He left James unsleeping but tucked in with an iron hand. Angela was nowhere to be seen. He called softly so as not to alert the boy. Floorboards creaked as he moved about: his reflection in a mirror showed a big man tiptoeing and looking sheepish.

He tapped on her bedroom door, spoke softly. 'Angela, I'm going.'

Suddenly she was behind him: she had come from the bathroom, holding a bathrobe round her. By accident or design the robe fell open when she made a hasty movement. For a split second they gazed, he at her nakedness, she at his face as it suffused with colour. Then she snatched the robe together, turned her back.

He said, 'I'm sorry—'

'Don't apologise, it's humiliating.'

'It's my fault – not being organised.'

'*Organised*?' She uttered that dry sound in her throat again.

'An affair of this sort – and this more than most, because we're such near neighbours – requires careful planning – orchestrating.'

'Affair?'

'Clandestine.'

'Is that how you see it? I'm to be your little bit on the side?'

Owen protested, 'Is that how it seems?'

'Don't worry, I shan't harass you. Greville's coming back.'

Owen said, 'Good. You've sorted things out between you?'

'Not quite everything.' She was plaiting her hair as she spoke. 'I'm going to stay with my mother in Friern Barnet.'

'Think about it; don't make up your mind on the spur of the moment.'

'This moment has plenty of spur.' She smiled wryly.

'What about James?'

'Greville agrees he must go away to school: it's best we don't try to share his upbringing.' She drew the finished plait over her shoulder. 'I still love my husband, you know.'

Owen, who hadn't known, was glad. He had wanted to leave her with something. Hope could be recognised without being guaranteed.

He set a match to the heap in the garden. The stuff on top had dried: a thread of black smoke came up from the base which was still damp. There was no fragrant woodsmoke, which he understood was the reward of an autumn bonfire.

At this time of year the garden had little to commend it. The grass looked chewed, the broad-leaved trees had been stripped by the first of the winter winds and stood as a black scribble against the sky. Owen found himself hankering after pavements, well-defined stone slabs with Nature pinned underneath; felt something like nostalgia for a whiff of London traffic.

He went to the garage, fetched newspapers and oily rags and pushed them into the bottom of the heap. The paper burned fiercely. Then the flames died. He went back to the garage, gathered the wood shavings and offcuts left over from his spell of carpentry. A wicker chair, left by the previous tenant, promised results. He carried it all to the heap which was putting up a wisp of black steam. He kicked it and the heap fell open on a nucleus of sweating twigs and charred rags. He heard a long-drawn hollow cry. Alarmed, he took a stick and stirred the embers. The cry came again, louder. James was behind him, carrying a bulky parcel.

'Hey, you gave me a fright. I thought, here's a firebird dropped into my bonfire, hoping to rise up young again from the ashes. It's an old Arabian custom.'

James giggled. Owen pushed the wood shavings into the heap and dropped the basket chair on top. He lit a match and held it to the shavings. They took at once: a ring of lusty flames spread and licked the old wickerwork of the chair. It was ablaze in a moment. James shouted for joy.

Owen said, 'What's in the parcel?'

James let it fall to the ground. Crouching, he tore off the brown paper and stood with his arms full of reddish fur. 'It's his coat.'

'Your father's?'

'The bear's coat. I've killed the bear.'

Solemnly he raised his burden and released it to the flames.

Antony found Pam piling clothes into a suitcase. 'What are you doing?'

'I want to go home.' Her lip trembled. Like a child's, he thought, his temper rising. 'I don't like being here—'

'You want to go home – I want to stay.'

'I can't go without you!'

'You can. We're not joined at the hip.'

'Nanty, you're not well, I know you're not. This place is bad for you. In the boat – I thought you were dying—'

'Disappointed, were you?'

'Nanty – don't!'

'You're the one that's sick. You and your plastic tadpole!'

He stormed out, slamming the door, and drove away fast. Clear of the Falmouth traffic, he plunged through everlasting lanes, past constantly recurring road junctions, grassy islands with finger-posts which he did not read. It didn't matter where he went, he needed to get away. If distance didn't make the heart grow fonder, it might help sort his feelings. Unprepared as he had been – or, rather, prepared for it to be nothing at all – when he looked over the side of the boat and saw that sheet of plastic stamped 'Blue Circle Cement Co.' he could have howled. Would he ever be able to make love to her without it coming between them? Turned off by a cement bag!

He cornered too sharply and finished on a grass verge,

front wheels just short of a ditch. He got out, locked the car and walked away, across a field.

The field had been left fallow. He found himself in a sea of wild flowers, buttercups, ox-eye daisies, dandelions, sheep's bit, foxgloves, laughing jacks. He watched his shoes turn yellow with pollen. Then the blossoming tide petered out.

He looked up. He had come to the edge of a wood. On the threshold, as it were, he was looking into a concourse of great trees, elms and oaks rejoicing as their leaves raced in the wind. Sunlight and shadow rocked the ground under his feet; the roaring of the leaves gathered strength from somewhere in the heart of the wood and deepened to a sustained organ note which swelled in his eardrums. He began to feel weightless, like nothing.

Pam might not be so wrong after all. The business with Soulsby was sheer kiddology, but this was how he had felt as he lay on his back in Clapham's boat. Perhaps he should get a medical check-up.

Driving back to the hotel he caught glimpses of the Carrick Roads. A yacht race was in progress, white sails running before the wind, sun sparkling off blue water – a picture from the calendar he had pinned over the sluice in the shop and kept tally of the days till their holiday. As a holiday it was a write-off. But at least – at most – it had clarified the situation between himself and Pam.

There had been life before her, but would he want it again? In his single existence he had spent a lot of time bar-crawling, seeking ad hoc girls. From that angle, the choice was clear.

He would be a fool to go back to random searching for a congenial partner.

I'll take her away, he thought, I'll ask no question, I'll go along with whatever she wants. This place brings out the morbid streak, but she's not the only one. There's Olssen painting monsters, Mrs Clapham attacked by her own saucepan, the Soulsbys are trying to work miracles and a deaf woman heard wolves.

Perhaps it depended on what was meant by miracles, how you look at them, and where. You shouldn't ask too much, a change of heart is a minor miracle.

The patrolman in the middle of the road seemed to be beckoning him on. He was waving his arms, his mouth opening, shouting. Antony slammed on his brakes, stalled the engine.

The patrolman, still waving his arms, ran to the car. He leaned in through the window.

'What's up?' said Antony.

'You can't come any farther. Go back.'

'Back where?'

'Back!'

The patrolman was very young, he still had a boy's fuzz on his cheek.

'I'm going to Falmouth,' said Antony.

'Take the M road.'

'Why should I? This is pleasanter.'

'There's a tree down, a great big tree . . .' He looked queer, his face was greenish and dewy with sweat.

'Don't worry, there are plenty more trees.'

'It's across the road. On top of a car!'

'Christ – is anyone hurt?'

The boy bit his lips, his jaw cracked. 'Two women . . .'

Antony reversed and drove away. He pulled up when he saw a man leaning on his cottage gate. 'What happened back there?'

'The old oak came down. I warned them. That tree's dangerous, I said, fixing to fall. I know, I said, owls, I said, have always lived in that tree. It's not easy for them to find roosts to suit them nowadays, they wouldn't go unless obliged to. They upped and left a week ago. That was a sign.'

'What happened? The patrol said a car was involved.'

'Built to last, those old cars were.' The man made an ugly face. 'This one won't.'

'Have they got the passengers out?'

'I don't reckon a flea could come out of that alive. They're waiting for lifting gear. They wouldn't let me near but I saw it under the tree.'

'Saw what?'

'An old bull-nosed Morris.'

Startled, Antony recalled a car parked alongside his at the Bellechasse. 'What was it like?'

'Like?'

'What colour?'

'Dark colour. It was pancaked, for God's sake.'

Antony had a vision which he would far rather not have had. He trod on the accelerator, tyres squealing, shot away.

Watch it, he told himself, this is where we came in, this is what it's good at, this place: intimidation, false alarms,

184

jiggery-pokery. At a rough estimate there was more than one vintage Morris in Cornwall. He had seen another only yesterday, resprayed shocking pink. Any number of them – golden oldies, bull-nosed and cherished – were bouncing along Cornish lanes at this minute.

His was the only car when he parked behind the Bellechasse, everyone else was out, everyone except Pam – waiting for him.

He ran upstairs calling her name. In their room was a letter written on one of the 'English Field Flower' series of notelets he had given her at Christmas: 'Nanty, I can't stay here. Senga's going back to London and is taking me. I'll be waiting for you at home.'